Tales
Of The
Wycked Aye
Tavern

By Maureen Arcuri &

Matt White

Tales of the Wycked Aye Tavern
1st Edition, 1st Printing – October 25, 2014
© 2014 By Maureen Arcuri & Matt White

I Street Press – **828 I Street, Sacramento, CA 95814**

Library of Congress No.: 204953729
ISBN: 978-1-941125-16-8

To Matt and David, Rose and Lance, St. Andrews
Noble Order of Royal Scots and the characters of the
Wycked Aye Tavern. This would never have
happened without you.

Maureen Arcuri

To Dad and all the stories I heard while I sat on the
porch as a boy.

Matt White

FORWARD

My dad was a wonderful storyteller and I was privileged to grow up listening to him. Story telling is the best and most ancient form of entertainment. It occurred to me that I might try my hand at this and tell stories about the characters of my renaissance reenactment group. I was surprised how much the stories were enjoyed, and was encouraged to write more. Along the way I met people, like Maureen, who also had a previously untapped talent for poetry and prose. What follows are the fruits of that collaboration first planted by my dad so long ago.

Matt White

Acknowledgements

To our Editor, Kim O'Donnell

To our Graphic Artists,

Karen Phillips and Lance Pyle

To our Publisher, Gerry Ward

Our Deepest Thanks to You All

Chapter One

For Katie

The Wycked Aye Tavern was busy this night. Everyone had gathered, for Philip and Maitiú had just returned from Skye and had many a tale to tell. Philip was out in the middle of it all, causing a ruckus as he always did. Maureen had been working in the tavern since the day Chieftain Heber had brought her there, filling pitchers and cleaning tables to earn her keep. She would always be grateful to Heber for bringing her to this place, and to Katie.

Katie MacLeod was born to Clan MacLeod on the Isle of Skye. Katie was Maureen's elder by eight years. Blue eyed and fair haired, Katie was a fine-looking woman; a strong, capable woman. She had grown up on Skye; all of her family was on Skye. When Katie met the wondering poet Philip MacAlasdair, they were married and she left Skye with him to live in the Scottish Highlands.

Maureen MacLeod was born on Skye but she did not grow up there. Her Father was a gallowglass, a Mercenary. When she was very young, he took her and her mother all the way across Scotland to the Lowlands near the English border. There he left them on a small piece of land owned by Clan Elliot and went off on campaign after campaign, fighting for money and anyone's cause that paid well. For years Maureen and her mother stayed on Elliot land tending a small herd of sheep and living a very secluded life. As the years passed, her father returned less and less, until he never came back: she and her mother had been abandoned. She was sixteen years old when the fever took her mother leaving her with no choice but to make her own way.

When the border disputes started up between the Armstrongs and the Elliots, she took her horse, Olaf, and left the hovel. She headed south to Dumfries with her mind set on begging passage on a ship out of The Solway and returning to Skye.

But she never made it to Dumfries. Caught in the middle of a clan war, she was taken by Clan Armstrong and forced into service in their household. She was treated with cruelty, as were all of the servants of the household. She suffered unspeakable abuses at the hands of old man Armstrong and his son.

The last time her master tried to take her against her will she would have none of it. Maureen found her strength; she found her pride and pulled her dagger. She cut old man Armstrong across his face. She was beaten and thrown in the stables. She ran from the house and fled her master's service. Taking her horse, she rode off into the night with nothing but the clothes on her back. They rode as far as they could until Olaf could go no further. Maureen and Olaf laid down in a meadow to rest. She was beaten, cold and hungry, but she was free from the torment of a vicious tyrant.

For almost a year she slowly worked her way north toward the Highlands and as far away from Clan Armstrong as she could get.

She found safe haven in the chapels and convents along the way. She loved the peace and beauty of the Mass, and found comfort in her faith. The priests and sisters would school her in reading and writing, and taught her the Gospels and the mystery of the Mass and Holy Communion.

She found work in the inns and taverns, cleaning, cooking and serving. She had no kin, no connections, no money and no home. She longed for a place to settle down and stop running.

When Chieftain Heber found her and Olaf taking shelter in his stable, she was scared, cold, painfully thin and her long auburn hair was full of straw. She reminded Heber of the old scarecrow in the tavern garden. He took pity on her and brought her to the Wycked Aye Tavern. When Maureen gave him her name, he took her to Katie and put her in Katie's charge to clean her up and put her to work. Maureen had never known any of her clan from Skye until she met Katie. It felt like she had been handed the home she had been missing for so long.

The Wycked Aye Tavern was just north of the border between the Highlands and the Lowlands, strategically located between Dumbarton and Sterling, and closer to Dumbarton near the River Leven. It was also near the crossroads to Edinburgh and Holyrood Castle. It was a large establishment originally owned by the MacGregors, but now it was the property of Dame Brittah Sutherland H'elie of

County Sutherland, which was far in the north of Scotland. She had named Heber MacPherson as her tavern chieftain to act as proprietor and oversee the business. Heber MacPherson never turned anyone away. He was a kind hearted man and always provided shelter and food to those in need.

But Heber's position encompassed far more than that. Though not a clan chieftain, he was the unspoken leader and advisor of all the surrounding lands—he was the eyes and ears of the Highlands.

The tavern was the central meeting place between the Highlands and the Lowlands, serving as a way station for those traveling to Dumbarton for passage by sea and traveling to Court at Edinburg, and the social gathering hall for the local folk of the shire. It was the hub for everyone traveling through Scotland.

The tavern had its own stable, livestock, farm and garden. It was not an inn, but did have a few cottages and small rooms available paying guests.

Katie was up front at the bar and Maureen was in back drawing ale from one of the kegs. Katie was not a regular worker at the tavern. She would help out when Philip was away to help pass the time or when extra help was needed for special occasions.

Maureen wasn't really paying attention until she heard Maitiú say her name to Katie.

"I checked on Maureen just like ya asked Katie," he said. "The old women of Skye, they remembered a MacLeod girl-child named Maureen. They said she be the child of one Robert MacLeod and that they disappeared years back and have nay been heard from since. Seems MacLeod was a gallowglass. He took the wife and girl-child with him on campaign and they never returned to Skye. 'Tis all I could find out fer ya." Katie thanked him quietly and he left.

Maureen was puzzled by what she had just heard. Why was Katie checking up on her? Did Katie not believe her to be of Clan MacLeod? If Katie was not sure about her, then the others were likely asking the same questions. In all truth, she could not blame any of them for their doubts. It's not every day when a young woman alone walks into a tavern claiming to be kin, looking to be nothing more than a starving little waif and not carrying a damn thing to her name.

Just then she heard Katie call from the bar, "Are ya fillin' those pitchers or drinkin' em girl?"

"I be bringin' 'em straight away, Katie," Maureen replied, and hurried back out into the tavern.

It was a long night at the tavern; a night of stories, laughter and song, and a lot of ale. So many goodly people they are, the Highlanders of this tavern. Perhaps if she could find something, anything from her family that she could give to Katie to prove herself a true MacLeod, maybe then Katie would believe her.

Heber's sister, Elena, put her arm around Maureen's shoulders and said, "A bit quiet ya are tonight girl, somethin' on yer mind?"

"Nay, Mistress MacPherson, ya know good 'n well that ya can nay get a word in edgewise with Philip tellin' his tales and Maitiú' singin' his songs."

Maureen wanted these people to know that she was true to her word. There was something different about this tavern, a warmth and comfort she had not known before. She wanted very much to stay with these people.

It would mean returning to the border. A place she had spent the last few years escaping. But it would be wrong to just leave and not say a word to anyone...she would think on it for a day or two and talk with Fionnula.

Fionnula MacPherson was wife to Chieftain Heber. She was also the cousin of Maitiú, the Irishman. Maltworm they called him, for the brew master he was. They had some other names for him as well. Names Maureen did not care for too much. She liked Maitiú; he was a good man, true to heart. Fionnula was very much like him, a kind and gentle woman, pretty, and a bit of a flirt. With flaming red hair and bright crystal blue eyes, she was a true ginger. But though she was still a young woman, she carried with her the wisdom of a sage.

In the two days that passed from that night at the tavern Maureen thought long and hard about traveling back to the border, back to the hovel where she and her mother had lived. She remembered, though she was very young at the time, her mother taking the coin her father had left with them and the few precious trinkets they had, putting them in a chest and burying them just up from the hovel. He had insisted that her mother hide it; Maureen never understood why. When her mother died of the fever and trouble started on the border, she fled without even a thought of looking for any of it. The hovel would surely be gone by now, but the marker should still be there.

It would be a risky trip, but worth it if she could find that chest. For the chest held a broach with the crest of Clan MacLeod. Their names were engraved on the back of it. She would find it and bring it back for Katie.

It was early in the afternoon when Maureen walked into the tavern. Akira Elliot, wife of Braden Elliot, was there keeping a watch over the Elliot children. Lord Cullen Elliot, Braden's brother, sometimes brought his wife Gwen and their daughter to the tavern when trouble was about. Elliot lands lay on the English border and times were not safe right now. Cullen had returned to defend his lands and left Gwen and his daughter under the watchful eye and ready swords of Chieftain Heber and his brother Braden.

Fionnula was behind the bar beginning to prepare food for the evening. Heber was Chieftain and proprietor of the tavern; as his wife, she was expected to help manage the day-to-day work. She looked up as Maureen approached.

"Ya be early lass but I be glad to see ya, I could use the help."

"There be something on me mind Fionnula, can we talk a bit?" Maureen shared with her what had happened in the tavern and what Maitiú had said to Katie.

Fionnula stopped what she was doing, put down her knife and let out a long sigh. "'T'as been a long time since Katie has been back to Skye and seen any of her Clan. She misses her own people. When ya appeared out of the blue, she was very happy to have one of her own clan with her. Do nay be too hard on her, lass. Maybe she just wants to be sure. Maybe she does nay want to be hurt—to get too close and then have ya disappear."

Maureen told Fionnula that she wanted to return to her home in Lowlands to get the few mementos from her family that were left behind. She told Fionnula that she would only be gone for a short while, four or five days at the most. That she was going back to the border to bring something back for Katie, and then she would have no doubts. Maureen was Clan MacLeod, of that she was sure, and when she returned everyone else would be sure of it as well.

Fionnula looked at her, crossed her arms over her chest and dropped her chin a bit.

"I do nay think it wise to be goin' off by yourself girl, especially off to the border, not now. Chieftain would nay approve," she said.

"Chieftain does nay need to know," Maureen replied. "And besides, I been on me own for a very long time, I can handle meself. I need to go back and get that chest. 'Tis all that be left of me family. I should never have left it behind."

At that, Fionnula shook her head and said, "You be just as stubborn as Katie, ya must be a MacLeod."

Maureen worked that night at the tavern; she would leave first thing in the morning.

Maureen was up early to saddle Olaf and be on her way. Heber allowed her to keep her horse, Olaf, stabled there. Olaf was a beautiful black stallion, named for Olaf the Black. Being alone for so long, he had been her only true friend for many years. He had wandered up to their hovel one day, starving and wounded. He still bared the scar of a deep sword wound on his hind quarter. She and her mother took him in and cared for him, and he had been with her

8

ever since.

Maureen was carrying her single hand long blade, her dirk and her doe-hoof dagger. She was nearly ready to ride when she heard footsteps behind her in the straw of the stable. She turned and saw it was Detta.

Detta worked the early hours at the tavern. She was a sweet thing, quieter than most of the women of the tavern. A tall, slender lass with long brown hair and dark eyes. She had a son, Merrick, a handsome young lad. She was by herself with the boy. No one was quite sure what became of her man. She had never shared that with anyone, nor had anyone ever asked her.

"So, ridin' out are ya?" she said.

"I have some business to take care of Detta; I be back in a few days."

"What kind of business are ya doin' that causes ya ta be carryin' three blades?" Detta asked.

"Can nay be too careful these days ya know," Maureen casually replied. Maureen could hear the concern in Detta's voice.

"Does Mistress Morna know ya be leavin'?"

"Nay" Maureen replied, "but Fionnula does."

"God speed girl." Detta said as she stepped away.

"Many thanks Detta, and please, da nay say anythin' to Katie." And with that Maureen mounted her horse and rode out.

She rode out at a good clip; the road would be quiet now. She would be on Elliot land in no time and back at the tavern before anyone noticed she was gone.

It was Mistress Morna who noticed Maureen missing that first afternoon. "Where be the other MacLeod this day?" she asked of Fionnula.

"She will nay be comin' in tonight Morna, might be a few days before she be back," she replied.

"She shoulda checked with me before leavin'. We have a tavern ta run ya know, and Detta can nay stay all night."

"I know Morna. We be managin' just fine," Fionnula replied. "She be back in a few days, she had some business to take care of near the border and..."

"Near what border?" It was Heber. Katie and Philip were right behind him.

"She be gone?" asked Katie. The concern and disappointment on Katie's face was obvious. Heber looked to his wife for explanation.

Fionnula knew there was no point in avoiding the truth. She had been married to Heber for years and he knew her far too well. She told Heber of her conversation with Maureen in the tavern. Then she told Katie that Maureen knew about Maitiú and Skye.

"This be all me fault," said Katie, "I be goin' after her."

"I be goin' with ya, Katie," said Philip.

"Enough!" shouted Heber. Everyone silenced immediately. He looked toward Braden and said, "We be goin' after her, she can nay be that far ahead of us." A little smile emerged across Braden's face. Braden Elliot was one of the finest swordsmen in the Highlands and a fierce warrior. He was Heber's right-hand man and he loved a good fight of any kind. And besides, he was an Elliot and knew his way about the Lowlands. Heber slapped Braden on the back of the head and said, "Get ready boyo. What say ya, we go find yer brother and then see if we can nay find our young Mistress Macleod."

The men gathered their swords from the weapons rack and as Heber approached the door to the tavern he turned, looked straight at Katie and said, "If one more MacLeod woman walks through this door, I be leavin' for good."

It was the end of the third day when Maureen arrived at the old path that led to the hovel. Years had passed since she had left. The land was as beautiful as she remembered. She first went to the place where, by her own hand, she laid her mother to rest. When she died, Maureen had waited as long as she could, hoping her father would return, but he never did.

Her mother's cairn was undisturbed and wildflowers had grown all around it. She was surprised to see that a bit of the old hovel remained. Not much, but enough to give her a landmark to work from. There, just off the corner and up the hill, was the marker: simply a stone set under the watchful bows of the great oak.

Low and behold, the chest was still there, wrapped in oilcloth and fairly well preserved. She quickly opened it and there was the broach, also wrapped in oilcloth, and a few other things as well: a smaller chest and some coin, and odds and ends.

She did not take the time to look too closely as the sun was setting and this was no place to be caught at night and alone. She quickly emptied the chest into her saddlebags, placed it back under the marker and covered it as best as she could.

She took one more look around, said a prayer to her mother, and left. She knew she would never return to this place again.

There was a small pub about two miles back down the road. She would take rest there tonight and begin her journey back to the Wycked Aye in the morning.

The little pub was busy and most turned to look as Maureen entered. Although many Highlander women carried blades, it was not usual to see a woman traveling alone and heavily armed. She found a small table, back out of the way. It was good to sit and rest.

The patrons were a mixed group. It was very near the borders of Clan Armstrong, Clan Elliot and England. It was noisy in the pub; so many conversations going on at once. A fire crackled in the fireplace and a thin layer of smoke floated above the tables. A pretty young woman moved through the crowd, serving ale and cleaning tables. The men would yank her arms and pull at her skirts. She looked tired and sad; Maureen knew exactly how she felt. When she asked if there was something Maureen wanted, she looked down at the dagger and said, "ya best be puttin' that out of sight; these men, they be lookin' for trouble."

"Many thanks fer the warnin' Mistress, I be careful" Maureen replied. "Mead, and some bread and cheese if ya please."

The mead and food were comforting. All seemed to be going well when from behind her she heard a voice say, "MacLeod, Maureen MacLeod."

A cold chill went down her back for she knew that voice well. It made her sick to her stomach. It was Ian Armstrong, the filthy toad of a man she never wanted to see or hear ever again.

"I was nay sure at first if it be you," he said. "Then I saw the doe-hoof." He walked around in front of the table. His right eye bore a nasty scar, compliments of Maureen's doe-hoof dagger. He moved around to her side of the table, put his fist in her hair and yanked her head back.

"Have a good look at your handy work, lass," he spat.

Maureen said nothing and started to reach for her blade. He yanked her head back farther, "Do nay do it lass, it will nay work this time. Ya owe me girl."

"I owe ya nothin' ya filthy toad, I told ya that before."

"Yer father took something from me lass and I want it back," he growled.

"I told ya before Armstrong, I do nay know what the bloody hell yer talkin' about. I do nay have anythin', and he never told me anythin'!" He yanked at her hair again and she let out a little screamed.

That brought the attention of the patrons and they began to move away from the table. The young barmaid tried to come to Maureen's aide, but Armstrong pushed her away and she tumbled to the floor.

Then there came a rustling of tables and the skidding of chairs. Out of the corner of her eye, Maureen could just see a man striding towards them from the front of the tavern, straight toward Armstrong.

13

Lord Cullen Elliot stood only a few feet from the table. His sheer presence commanded respect.

"Release her, Armstrong, and we be allowin' ya ta live through the night," he said. Armstrong did not move and he did not let go.

"This be not yer concern Elliot, this wench means nothin' ta ya. Leave me ta me business and be on yer way." He turned his attention back to Maureen, ignoring Cullen.

It seemed like forever, then finally she heard the familiar singing of swords as they were drawn from their scabbards. Chieftain Heber's sword was on Armstrong's throat before he could blink an eye. Cullen's blade was up against his chest. From behind, Braden's blade was square on Armstrong's back, pointed straight at his black heart. Armstrong released his grip and Maureen scrambled from her chair. Braden grabbed her arm and pushed her out of the way.

They led Armstrong out of the tavern on the points of their swords. What was said and done outside the door, Maureen did not know.

When Heber came back in, he simply looked at her and said, "Gather yer belongin's girl and get yer horse. We be havin' a talk when we get back to the Wycked Aye."

The three-day journey back to the Wycked Aye was tense but without incident. Maureen and Olaf rode behind the men, and she did her best to stay out of Heber's way when they stopped for the night. He was angry with her and she knew he would speak to her when he was ready. On the third day, the weather was in their favor and they arrived back in the shire in the early afternoon.

As they entered the tavern, Akira met Braden with a kiss. Fionnula embraced Heber. Katie and Philip came toward Maureen. Katie had tears in her eyes, as did Maureen.

She took Katie's hand and laid the broach wrapped in oilcloth in her palm. Katie opened it to reveal the Crest of Clan MacLeod. On the back were the names Robert, Maire and Maureen.

"'Tis beautiful," Katie said softly.

"I want ya to have it Katie; a gift from MacLeod to MacLeod."

"Ya did nay have to go all that way just to bring this to me," Katie scoffed.

"Ah, but I did. You be all I have now Katie, I want ya ta trust me." And with that Maureen turned to leave the tavern. As she passed by Heber, he reached over and grabbed hold of her arm. She looked up and said "I know Chieftain, we be havin' a talk."

When she arrived back in her little room at the stable, she took the saddlebag and dumped it out on the table. She had not taken the time to look through it until now. Most of it was familiar to her. A small amount of coin, a ring that was her mother's. But the small chest, she did not remember. The ride back in the saddlebags had caused it to break into pieces. It contained two leather pouches. When she opened them, she damn near fell off her chair.

"Mary, Mother of God," she whispered to herself. The first was full of gold and the second full of gemstones: red, green and white stones. So this is why her father had wanted it hidden away. Dear God, this is what Armstrong was after all along! It looked as if she and the Chieftain would be talkin' about a few more things than he expected.

Chapter Two

Heber's Judgment

Maureen's trip to the border had left her feeling a bit melancholy. Her mind was racing with questions. She stayed in her little chamber for a day or so wondering about her father, for it was clear to her now he was not the honorable man she had once thought him to be. He was a Gallowglass, a ruffian and a thief. As she sat in her chamber pondering so many questions that she would never have answers to, she had been idly fiddling with the broken pieces of the chest that had held the bag of gold and jewels. She was moving the bits of wood around like pieces to a puzzle. When she got the pieces back together, she could see that at one time the chest had been beautifully adorned with paint and inset gold. The chest bore a Coat of Arms, one she did not recognize. It mattered not. It was just one more piece to a puzzle far too big for her to solve.

It was time to put all of this behind and move on. She had Katie and Philip, and the goodly folk of the Wycked Aye. Looking for answers to the past would only bring trouble and heartache. She would take the

gold, the jewels and the chest to Chieftain Heber;
whatever his counsel would be, it would be final.

Have ya seen her at all Katie?" asked Elena. The
women were busy in the tavern that afternoon as
always.

"Nay, I've not. I thought I'd give the girl a bit of
time alone" Katie replied. "She's been through a bit ya
know and might need some time to think it through."

Fionnula came forward and put a hand on Katie's
shoulder. As Katie turned to her she said, "Ya need to
go fetch Maureen, Katie; Chieftain wants to see her—
now."

The Chieftain was seated to the back of the tavern
by the fire at "his" table. The great table he had
specially made, just for himself. Although the table
was in a common area of the tavern, it was placed back
away from the others; back where Heber could meet
and talk away from the ears of the patrons, a place for
bartering and negotiation with the leaders of other
Clans. Many came to the Chieftain for counsel for he
was a wise and even-handed man.

Maureen waited back away from the table for
Heber to see her and bid her to come forward. For no
one had leave to invite himself to Heber's table, unless
he was a bloody fool. Chieftain finally looked up and
beckoned her forward. He pointed to the bench
directly across from him and she quietly took her
place.

"I hope ya understand that yer little trip to the
border has stirred up a bit of a hornet's nest. Master
Armstrong seems to be of a mind that ya be in

18

possession of somethin' of great value to him...and he be wantin' it back." Heber paused for a moment. She knew it was not her time to speak and that he would tell her when it was; he was choosing his words carefully. He continued, "Lord Elliot and meself have informed Armstrong that ya know nothin' of it and to leave it be. Whatever that father of yers did, 'tis long past and best be forgotten. Ya know lass, the Armstrongs be a large and powerful clan. I do nay need trouble from a clan like that; Lord Cullen does nay need trouble from a clan like that. So, I trust this be the end of it?"

Maureen could not speak. He just stared, awaiting a response. He had to know; she owed him the truth and nothing less. She pulled the satchel from her lap and laid it on the table. His eyes narrowed as he said, "What this be all about, lass?"

Maureen began her story about the chest with the gold and jewels. When she had finished, she looked her Chieftain in the eyes and said, "I swear to ya Chieftain, on me mother's grave, I dinnae know these were in the chest." And with that, she opened the satchel and dumped out the gold and jewels on the Chieftain's table.

"God's teeth, girl," he said as he quickly covered the pile of wealth with the satchel cloth. A few heads turned to look as the bounty clattered on the top of the table. He waited until all had gone back about their business before he raised the cloth for a better look. As he separated the coin from the jewels he said quietly, "Who knows of this?"

"No one knows, only you," she replied.

"Not even Katie?" he said with a bit of a raise to his voice. For he knew if she would tell anyone, she would tell Katie.

"Nay, not even Katie. I swear it." He continued to count and they both sat in silence. Only the crackling of the fire and the muffled conversations of the tavern filled the room. As Maureen could stand the silence no longer, she finally asked him, "I have never seen coin like this before, I know not what it be or what it be worth. Do ya know what they be Heber?

"Aye, I do indeed," he said as he let out a long sigh. "These be English fine sovereign, fifty pieces of fine sovereign...a bloody fortune to someone like you or me."

"Do ya think this be what that filthy toad Armstrong be after?" she asked. The Chieftain only nodded. It was time to put the last card on the table. She brought forth the pieces of the broken chest. "This be what they be packed in," and she began to reassemble the pieces to form the coat of arms painted on the top of the chest. Heber watched with curiosity and she could tell by his expression that he did not recognize this standard.

"Do ya know where it came from?" she asked.

"Nay Mistress MacLeod, I know not." He was troubled, it was plain to see.

"What be your counsel Chieftain, I be doin' whatever ya say," as she lowered her eyes to await his decision. Before he said a word, he gathered the pieces of the broken chest and pitched them into the fire.

"Gather up yer dowry girl. Take it back to yer chamber and hide it well." Then he raised his voice for all to hear and said, "then get yer troublesome MacLeod arse back over here and get to work." He raised his cup of ale and drained it down. As he lowered his tankard, his eyes came straight into hers, "Now, walk yerself out of here as if not a thing be on yer mind and be back straightaway. I need to seek counsel of another. Do nothin' with any of this until I return. Now go, off with ya."

"As ya wish Chieftain," and with a proper bow of her head, she did exactly as he asked.

It was good to get back to the day-to-day routine of the tavern. All was perfectly normal for the next few days. It was spring in the Scottish Highlands, but the weather had turned unseasonably cold. The skies had darkened and a storm was on the way. The tavern was full of local patrons and weary travelers seeking a warm fire and cup of fine ale.

All kinds came to the Wycked Aye Tavern, Chieftain rarely turned anyone away. On any one night you could hear talk of politics, clan disputes, news of Court and always debates on religion. Most of the time the discussions were peaceful and kept between the parties involved. But, like any place where people gather to talk, there were the people who had been sent just to listen. The threat of spies from England, Norway, France, Ireland and even the Queen herself were always present. People sent to sit and listen to the talk of others. The girls of the Wycked Aye were asked to listen as well, for their safety and the safety of the tavern.

For two nights in a row, the same two men dressed as country gentlemen had wandered into the tavern and taken the same table. The first night, they went fairly unnoticed by the workers of the tavern. The second night they asked Elena about her clan, where she was from. They both had eyes for Detta, and were making foul remarks to all the lasses, for though they were dressed in fine breaches and doublets, they did not speak or behave as gentlemen should. Katie and Philip were in the tavern that night. Katie pulled Maureen aside and warned her not to go near their table. These gents had plenty of coin and were getting their fill of ale.

"Ya go through almost as many women as Bothwell" said one.

"Well, at least I do nay promise to marry 'em and then leave 'em high and dry," said the other.

"Aye, the good Earl must have balls of solid rock to have gotten away with that one."

"Can ya imagine, promisin' a Norwegian nobleman that yer going to marry his daughter, bringin' her to the lowlands of Scotland and leavin' her there? The poor woman had to give up her entire chest of gold and jewels to buy passage back to Norway, and on one of Bothwell's ships no less," the two men rolled with laughter and called for another round of ale.

Maureen had heard tell of this Earl of Bothwell; the "enemy of all good men" they called him. Handsome and powerful he was. He would stop at nothing if it would put gold in his pocket or better his position. He even changed his religion when it suited his purpose. But that was not the part of the story that caught her attention, it was the dowry of the Norwegian noble woman.

Mistress Morna was uneasy with these strangers in the tavern for they did not seem to be waiting for someone else to arrive. They seemed to be watching her girls. She moved to the back of the bar and whispered to Heber, "They be back again tonight

Heber. They keep askin' the lasses questions 'bout their homes, their clans. I do nay like it and the lasses are fed up with 'em. Elena be ready to run 'em through and if she does nay do it, I be pretty sure Connor will".

"I had me eyes on them as well, Mistress Morna," said Heber with a lowered voice. "I know not who they be, but I believe I know who sent them. I be leavin' first thing come mornin' for the Lowlands to finish this matter once and for all. Go to them Tánaiste, fill their cups and send them to me table." He filled his tankard with ale and returned to his table.

Morna approached the men and topped off their tankards, "Good gentles, the Chieftain bids ya join him at his table," she said. The two strangers glanced to each other and back to Morna. She said nothing back, just pointed the way to the big man's table and walked away.

The two men turned their gaze to the Chieftain. They rose slowly and moved toward the big man's table for they now had the attention of not only the Chieftain, but also that of Braden, Connor and Philip.

Katie snagged Maureen by the back of her bodice and yanked her into the back of the tavern, putting a finger to her lips to stay quiet. As the two strangers began to seat themselves at Heber's table, the Chieftain spoke.

"Do nay sit! What I have ta say will nay take long. I know not yer names lads, but I believe I know who sent ya." The larger of the two men interrupted.

"We be here for the wench called MacLeod, the one who wears the doe-hoof dagger. Turn her over and we be makin' it worth yer while, and leave ya in peace." Heber bolted to his feet, slamming his hands on the table.

"Ya have no barterin' rights at this table, boyo."
Heads turned and a hush fell throughout the tavern.

"Now, I bid ya return to yer Master Armstrong, tell him I be meetin' him in three days' time at the same place we had our last little talk. And if I ever hear either of ya speak of tradin' Highlander women as if they be cattle, I be runnin' ya through meself. Now leave me tavern and never return, yer no longer welcome here."

The larger man began to speak, then thought better of it. The two men turned to find themselves flanked by Connor, Braden and Philip. Everyone watched quietly as they moved through the tavern. They gathered their belongings and left the Wycked Aye.

As the door closed behind them, Heber caught the attention of Connor. A slight tilt of his head gave Connor his instructions: follow the men and make sure they were well on their way. Connor nodded back, and then quietly slipped out the back of the tavern. As he passed by, he gave both Katie and Maureen a stern look, and then he was gone.

Morning broke under a sky of grey. The air was strangely still; there was no movement about—no birds singing, no rustling of the little creatures in the grass and bushes. It was a sure sign that the Earth Mother was bringing a storm this way. Connor arrived just as Heber was finishing packing his horse.

"I followed them well past Linton. They're runnin' with their tails betwixt their legs, Heber. They should be well over the River Tweed by now and on their way to Selkirk."

"Well met, Connor. Keep an eye on the tavern won't ya lad. I be back as soon as this matter is settled."

Fionnula approached her husband with a small bundle of food for the journey. "Do ya have to be goin' off now husband? The weather is turnin' foul and Maitiú should be here any time with the barrels of ale from Desmond. I do nay want ya to go Heber, I have an ill feelin' about it." Fionnula pleaded with him not to go.

"Ah wife, you and yer Irish intuition. Do nay worry on it woman, it be just a rain storm. It be passin' by and I be back before ya know it. Connor and Braden are here to help Maitiú with the ale." He embraced his wife, mounted his horse and set out for the border.

Heber had told Fionnula of the need for this trip as soon as he knew of the gold and jewels. She was his wife and he knew he could trust her. She knew he would be meeting with Lord Cullen near Selkirk to seek his counsel, and then continuing to the border of Elliot land to deal with Armstrong. Connor and Fionnula walked back to the Wycked Aye together. The air was growing colder. Connor put his arm around Fionnula as she shivered.

"He be fine Fionnula, ya need nay worry, Heber can take care of himself," he said trying to ease her mind.

"I know that Connor, that be not what has me bothered, 'tis the storm."

Maureen stayed through the night with Katie and Philip. Philip had insisted that she not return to her chamber alone.

Philip MacAlisdair was a poet and performer. He made his living entertaining people with his poetry and stories. He was a distinguished looking man, with dark hair greying at the temples, and a full beard. Philip held to the old ways of the forest. He rejected the organized religions of men and held to pagan ways of the ancient Gaels. He had met Katie while performing his poetry on Skye. Their match was not well received by Clan MacLeod and so Philip brought Katie back to the Highlands. He made his home in the shire, as it provided a central place for him to travel around Scotland performing.

Maureen awoke to the sound of Philip building a fire in the cottage. It was cold, very cold for spring. They sat near the hearth, sipping a warm cup of tea and talking of the weather and storms of the past. Katie was working on her needlework as always. Katie's skill with needle and thread was well known throughout many shires of the Highlands. She made a fair income with her stitchery and only worked at the tavern now and then. Maureen liked to tease Katie, telling her that there was Fairie magic from Skye in her needles. Katie would always just laugh, saying that Fairie magic was nothing but horse apples.

"I just do nay understand why that blaggard Armstrong still be tailin' after ya Maureen. Why will he nay leave ya alone?" she asked.

"I do nay know Katie" Maureen replied. "I know not what went on between me Da and Armstrong, maybe when those ruffians return empty handed, he'll leave it be." She left it at that. She did not think it wise to make Katie privy to the gold and jewels just yet. Heber wanted it kept secret for now, and that is how it would stay until he decided otherwise. She turned the conversation back to women's talk. Katie was helping her with her embroidery and needlework.

As they laughed and talked, Philip went to bring in a bit of wood for the fire. From outside the door they heard him call, "Lasses, come and have a look at this." Katie and Maureen went to the door and there stood Philip, his arms spread wide. Beautiful flakes of white were silently floating down from the sky all around him. It was snowing.

Maureen gathered her things and headed back to her chamber. She was due at the Wycked Aye by mid-afternoon, and she still had chores to attend to and animals to care for at the stables. The snow had begun falling in the early morning and showed no signs of stopping. It was a chilly ride back, but beautiful to see. Children laughed and played in the snow, using this most unusual storm as a time for celebration. As she rode past the Wycked Aye, there was a great commotion for Maitiú had arrived from Desmond with the barrels of ale. That brought a smile to her face. She liked that crazy Irishman - he made her laugh.

Maitiú Mac Roibeard de Faoite, Brew Master for the Earl of Desmond, was the cousin of Fionnula MacPherson and also Lady Gwendolyn Elliot. He was also a long-time friend of Philip MacAlisdair. Fionnula had arranged a contract for Maitiú with Heber to provide the tavern with all of its ale. Although Maitiú was Fionnula's kin, he did not usually receive too warm a welcome from the folks of the Wycked Aye, for he was Irish and Catholic, and many did not take to those who held to the Church of Rome. But he had a good heart and true spirit.

Maitiú was of average stature, not a big man like Heber, with brown hair and brown eyes. He was lean and fit, with the frame of a runner. The bogtrotter they called him, for the man did love to run. He was establishing a brewery in the shire, backed by the Earl of Desmond, to brew the Desmond ale along with many other fine brews of his own design.

Maureen had met Maitiú at Mass when she first arrived in the shire, and then again at the tavern. They had become friends immediately as they shared something in common – their faith.

The tavern would be busy tonight for the Desmond ale was something special. Heber had run off those nasty Lowlanders, Maitiú was here, the ale was here and it was snowing.

By the time Maureen got back to the Wycked Aye, the snow was building up on the ground and the flakes were still falling. As she entered the tavern her heart leapt with joy for there was Faolan leaning on the bar talking to Grady. Faolan was one of the many lost souls (like Maureen) that Fionnula and Heber had taken under their wing. Faolan had been away looking for work where he could find it.

"Faolan me friend," she shouted as she hurried to the bar to greet him. She threw her arms around his neck and he picked her up by her waist, swinging her around before setting her back on her feet.

"Hello lass" he said. "I be glad to see ya made it back from the border alright". How did he know she had gone down to the border? She looked behind the bar at Elena.

"Aye, I told him the whole story of yer little trip south that damn near got ya killed," she said rather matter-of-factly and with a bit of a grin on her face. Elena was a woman of few words. She never beat around the bush about anything. "And if I nay be mistaken, are ya nay supposed ta be workin' here tonight?"

"Aye, Elena, that I am," Maureen said with a smile.

"Morna's waitin' for ya in back," she said, "'tis going to be a long night with the storm and all."

Maureen turned to Faolan, "Can we talk later? Will ya be around for a while?" she asked. He smiled and nodded his head.

The news of the arrival of the Desmond ale had spread through the shire and the tavern was full to the brim. Maitiú and Connor were behind the bar singing one of Maitiú's Irish ditties.

Hands were clapping and tankards were clinking. Fionnula was as busy as the rest of the girls, but she did not seem herself. It was then Maureen realized that the Chieftain was not there. When she finally had a moment between pouring ale and pulling lamb out of the fire, she managed to catch Fionnula alone.

"Fionnula, where be the Chieftain? Are ya alright, ya seemed a bit troubled?"

"Heber has gone to Selkirk to seek counsel with Lord Elliot as to how to deal with those little bags of trouble yer Da left for ya," she said. Her tone was sharp.

"I be so sorry Fionnula, 'twas not me intention to bring any kind of trouble to the tavern," Maureen said quietly. "I thought it best that the Chieftain know what be goin' on. Ya know I be most grateful for all ya've done fer me."

Fionnula turned to her and with a deep sigh, cupped Maureen's face in her hands. Maureen could feel the kindness and gentleness of her spirit in her touch. "Ah, 'tis not yer fault lass, do nay worry over it. Heber will set things to right, I have no doubt of that. 'Tis just this storm, 'tis so strange and I just have an ill feelin'."

"You women and yer intuition, 'tis hard to know if it be a blessin' or a curse." It was Faolan. "What's got ya troubled, Mistress MacPhearson, I be at yer service to cure all yer woes M'lady," and he bowed gracefully to Fionnula. That made her smile. She did not answer him, she just gave Faolan a warm embrace and went back to work at the tables.

Faolan turned to Maureen and asked, "What be troublin' our goodly Mistress?"

"Ya know Fionnula, sometimes she has a feelin' about things. Heber has gone to Selkirk to meet with Lord Elliot and she be worried about him being caught in the storm I think."

Faolan looked at her with a blank expression on his face. "Selkirk, are ya sure? he asked.

"Aye, I be pretty sure. Faolan what be wrong?"

"I just came up from the lowlands. Both Lord Bothwell and Argyll are there on business. They both be travelin' north, comin' up from Armstrong land. 'Twould not be good for the three of them to come together."

He was right. If Heber was traveling south and the other two north, there was only one main road that they would be using. Maureen looked at Faolan and said "Fionnula's ill feelin' was right, we have to go after Heber."

Heber and Lord Cullen's meeting with Armstrong was stern and brief. It was made very clear to the lowlander that he and his ruffians were not to return to the Wycked Aye. As Heber and Cullen began their trip back, the skies overhead began to darken and snow began to fall.

"Damn," he thought to himself, "shoulda listencd to the wife after all." They rode on until the snowfall became too heavy to continue. There was a tavern just up ahead; Heber would take refuge there until the storm cleared. Lord Cullen would have time to return home ahead of the worst of the storm. He rode along with Heber to make sure he had shelter for the night before riding back to his own lands.

As Heber brought his horse up to the sheltered stable next to the tavern, he saw smoke coming from the chimney. He walked his horse around and tied him to a hitch in one of the stable stalls. As he walked around to the front of the stable, he noticed two fine coaches and one carriage, as well as two other horses that were stabled.

"Good, plenty of company to share an ale with," he thought. But when he looked closer at the coaches, he saw they bore the standards of Clan Hepburn and Clan Campbell. He was instantly on his guard. Cullen was waiting on his horse in front of the tavern.

"God's teeth, what be the chances of this," he said to Cullen.

Archibald Campbell, Earl of Argyle, was a man of affluence and known throughout Scotland. He was a devout Calvinist and had a vision of a united kingdom of Scotland and England under Scottish rule.

James Hepburn, Earl of Bothwell, on the other hand, was one of those Protestants who supported the "Auld Alliance" and the return of the young queen. Bothwell was a Protestant to be sure, but he was a Scotsman first and foremost.

Way up in the Highlands, the old clan systems still prevailed. A clan leader was not to lord his authority over his fellow clansmen. He was viewed as responsible for the wellbeing of his people. That was how Heber MacPherson was raised to believe and behave. He imposed no religious beliefs or political views upon anyone.

"Will ya be alright in there Heber?" Cullen asked.

"Aye, I believe I can hold me own, but send word to me wife of me delay, will ya now Cullen?"

Lord Cullen bowed his head in agreement and went on his way. Heber had no choice but to go in and wait out the storm—he could not continue in these conditions. But being in the same tavern with James Hepburn and Archibald Campbell would be a test of both his patience and his politics. He could only hope that the storm would end soon and that he could be on his way.

As he pushed open the door to the tavern the conversations began to quiet as the people came to recognize the Chieftain. Everyone knew who was in the tavern, and they waited to see how this confrontation would play out.

Heber quickly felt the mood in the room change as voices lowered to a whisper and the patrons' glances jumped from Heber to the table where the two Earls were seated. Heber walked to the back of the tavern and found a small table near the fire, a place where he could sit with his back to the wall and see the activity of the entire room.

Archibald Campbell was the first to speak. "Well, well, will ya look at this? It be the MacPherson himself. Come Heber, join us for an ale. Barkeep, bring two more tankards, one for each hand."

It was clear to Heber that they had been at the tavern for quite some time and had already consumed a few tankards of ale.

Heber bowed his head in acceptance and reluctantly joined them at their table. Slowly the conversations resumed as it seemed there would be enough ale to keep these three fellows content for the long evening ahead. The barkeep promptly brought the two tankards of ale for Heber. He knew that the gentlemen had plenty of coin and could make this night a very profitable one for his tavern.

"So, tell me Heber," continued Campbell. "What brings ya to the Lowlands?"

"I had a bit of private business to attend to down by the border M' Lord," replied Heber.

"And what kind of urgent business would a Highlander have in the Lowlands that would bring him out in such a storm? Is that blaggard Armstrong givin' ya trouble again MacPherson?" James Hepburn offered. Heber was not able to hide the surprise on his face.

"Do nay look so surprised Heber, I know what goes on in me own lands. Armstrong told me about his little skirmish with you and Elliot."

Heber did not respond. He waited for Hepburn to continue. After a short silence Hepburn laughed, "Armstrong is a pain in me arse as well, MacPherson.

33

Drink your ale man, do nay worry yerself over it."
Heber did just that.

The snow had fallen steadily. All of the women stayed through the night at the Wycked Aye to help for many had been stranded by the storm. As dawn was breaking, a messenger came bursting through the door.

"Mistress Fionnula MacPherson," he called. "I bring word from Lord Cullen Elliot. He wishes ya to know that the storm has struck the lowlands and Chieftain Heber is waiting for it to clear in a small tavern south of Selkirk near the border. He be in the company of the 4th Earl of Bothwell and the Earl of Argyle."

Everyone turned to look at Fionnula. They all knew that this was not a good situation. Most of the men had returned to their homes with their wives and little ones to weather the storm. Connor & Elena had gone, as well as Braden and Akira. Only Maitiú, Faolan and Philip remained along with some weary patrons.

Fionnula moved quickly to wake Maitiú. "Maitiú, Maitiú, wake up cousin!" she cried. "We need to be gettin' a carriage harnessed and go after Heber."

Maitiú shook his head and tried to rub the ale out of his eyes. "No, no, no. We can nay take the carriage, it will never get through. With all the snow on the road it will be nothin' more than a rutted, muddy mess. Give me a bit of time cousin, I have an idea how to get to Heber. I be back straight away Fionnula, do nay worry". Maitiú went over to Philip and slapped him on the head, "come along Philip, I be needin' some help".

Philip groaned and pulled himself up to follow Maitiú. Both had enjoyed themselves to the fullest the night before, and had drank a good amount of the Desmond ale.

When Maitiú and Philip returned about an hour later there was a great commotion when they arrived. Everyone went out to see what was going on. They were standing in front of the most curious contraption. It was a carriage of sorts, but with runners where the wheels should be. A sleigh Maitiú called it, and harnessed to the front was one of Maitiú's small Irish Connemara ponies. Connemara's were short and stout horses, well fitted for traveling through the bogs and mud. The men were crowded around the sleigh, loading a barrel of the Desmond ale on board. Everyone crowded around for a better look.

Maureen came around to the front of the sleigh to check on Grace, Maitiú's pony. Grace was one of the horses she cared for at the stables and she wanted to check her harnesses before they left. When she looked back at the front of the sleigh, she noticed a Coat of Arms painted on the front—the very same standard that was painted on top of the chest of gold and jewels. She immediately grabbed Maitiú by the arm.

"Maitiú, where did ya get this sleigh, where did it come from?"

"I traded for it a few years back from a party of Norwegian nobles. Seemed they were in need of a quick sale and it looked like a good way to move me ale in foul weather. Was nay sure if I would ever need it for anythin', but I be damn glad I have it now."

Norwegian, the Coat of Arms belonged to Norwegian nobility. Maureen's mind was swirling when...

"Maureen, Maureen," Faolan was calling to her. "Where be yer mind girl?

She turned to see Maitiú getting ready to take the sleigh and head off to get Heber.

"Wait," she called. "Maitiú, you should nay be the one to go south after Heber. The Lowlands are home to the Protestants and the Calvinists. They would nay take kindly to an Irish Catholic bringin' Irish ale to barter with. They be stealin' yer ale and stringin' ya up for certain."

"She be right," said Faolan. "I be the one ta go and get Heber". No one argued with Faolan's decision. Although Faolan was slight of build, he was a fine swordsman and could handle any situation. Besides, he had just come up from the Lowlands and had a good idea where to find Heber.

When morning came, the skies had cleared in the Lowlands. As the sun broke through the windows of the Lowland tavern, Heber awoke to the sound of bells. He had been at the tavern with the two Earls for two days now, waiting for the storm to clear.

"Good Lord, did I drink meself to death," he thought. The other folk in the tavern, as well as the two Earls, were also roused by the sound of bells. They followed the sound outside to see Faolan pulling up on the Norwegian sleigh with a barrel of Desmond Ale strapped to the back.

"Faolan lad, what are ya doing here and what the hell are ya ridin' on?" Heber asked as he rubbed the ale from his eyes.

"The goodly Mistress MacPherson sent me to fetch ya Chieftain. She sent the ale in case we needed to barter for your release."

The tavern owner was thrilled to see the barrel of Desmond ale, but his delight was promptly doused by the good Earl of Bothwell.

When James Hepburn saw the sleigh that Faolan was driving he was noticeably uncomfortable. "Tell me lad, where did ya acquire that sleigh of yers," asked Hepburn.

"Borrowed it from an Irish bogtrotter Your Grace," replied Foalan." The Earl questioned him no further.

Heber took immediate note of Hepburn's reaction, as he too recognized the Coat of Arms on the sleigh. There was an awkward silence between the three men. Heber moved quickly as he and Foalan, with the help of one of the Earl's footmen, moved the barrel of Desmond ale to one of Hepburn's wagons.

"There ya be M' Lord. That should make for a fine time at Hermitage Castle. I thank ya both for yer company and bid ya farewell." Heber bowed respectfully to the two Earls, as did Foalan.

"Come Foalan, we be on our way back to the Wycked Aye now. I trust me good Earl that you be rememberin' the generosity of the Wycked Aye Tavern shown to ya this day?"

"I will indeed MacPherson, I will indeed," replied Hepburn.

The storm had passed and the sky was clear when Faolan and the Chieftain arrived at the Wycked Aye. What a sight it was to see, the two Scots in a Norwegian sleigh being pulled by a stubby, Irish pony. All of the goodly folk of the Wycked Aye were there to welcome the Chieftain home and hardy cheers went out to Faolan for a job well done. There were hugs and warm wishes all around. As the Chieftain embraced his wife he whispered, "Next time I be payin' a bit more attention to yer intuition wife. There may be a bit of Fey in ya after all."

Everyone began to wander back into the tavern for the air was brisk and the warmth of the fire in the tavern was comforting.

Philip called out, "Can I draw ya an ale, Chieftain?"

"Nay Master Philip," Heber responded. "After bein' snowed in with the two Earls, I believe I've had me fill fer a bit. And from the look of you two," addressing Philip and Maitiú, "I be guessin' those barrels of the Desmond are empty? And I suppose me cash box contains its usual slip of parchment from Maitiú?"

"Nay Brother," chimed Elena. "He paid fer every tankard, I made sure of it."

"Well met Elena." Heber turned to Maitiú, "Ya pay her, but ya do nay pay me?"

"Aye," said Maitiú, "I be afraid of her." That brought laughter from everyone, including Heber.

Maureen waited as long as she could before she approached the Chieftain. He saw her coming toward him and motioned for her to come forward. Connor and Braden were at the big man's table as well.

Heber simply turned to her and said, "He be botherin' ya no more lass, 'tis over and done. Lord Cullen and Lady Gwen will be here in a few days, I believe we have a solution to yer problem. So, pour yerself some mead now, and spend some time with Faolan and the rest of the fine people of this tavern, for all be well in the Highlands this night!"

"But Heber, what about..." he stopped her.

"Ya asked for me judgment when ya came to me lass and me judgment ya shall have, but not tonight."

38

Chapter Three

The Warning

Pinterest.com

Oh, my aching head. That bloody Maitiú and his Irish whiskey, try it Maureen, you be likin' it, he said. Well, I nay be likin' it now! Maureen thought to herself. She felt like she had pipes playing in her head. She was certain Maitiú and Philip were having a good laugh at her expense this morning. She turned to look out the window of her chamber, but the sun hurt her eyes.

She realized that she was still in her clothes from last night, and someone had loosened the laces on her bodice. Dear God, it looked like she would be joining Maitiú in confession again. She managed to get herself up and pour a basin of water to bathe in. The cool water felt good on her face. She looked out the window, it appeared to be around late morning. Blast, she had overslept and had chores to do before heading over to the Wycked Aye. She dressed as quickly as she could with her head aching and the floor spinning, and headed to the stables. Besides working at the tavern, she cleaned the stables and fed the horses every morning in exchange for her room and board.

"Good mornin' me beauty," she said to Olaf. "I be certain yer feelin' better than I be this day." She fed him the carrot she brought for him every morning. He gobbled it down and tossed his head in thanks.

"Best be getting' to work, aye? Maybe this afternoon we can take a bit of a ride. I believe the fresh air would be doin' us both some good."

It took Maureen longer than she had expected. She had to stop and sit now and again, as her poor stomach was not in any way its regular self, and behaving quite strangely.

It was not as if she was a stranger to the taking of spirits. Since her mother passed, she had been on her own and working in taverns all over the Lowlands to earn her keep. She greatly enjoyed partaking in a cup of mead now and again. But this, dear God, this whiskey of Maitiú's, it felt like poison.

By the time she made it over to the tavern it was mid-day. As she came through the door everyone turned to look and then started to laugh.

"Well, well, look who's here, it be the life of the party," it was Elena. "Ya certainly had quite a time last night. I never knew ya could dance like that."

Dance...dance? Maureen did not remember any dancing. And why was Elena yelling at her, it made her head pound. Elena noticed Maureen cringe at her voice.

"Yer head givin' ya fits girl?" she said. Maureen did not answer her. She was so confused and embarrassed. She looked over to the bar and there sat Maitiú. He would not turn around, but she could see his shoulders bouncing from laughter.

40

Mistress Morna came out from the back of the bar, "Well, glad to see ya have straightened up a bit. Do ya think ya be able to finish yer work this night and not have to be carried home?" Maitiú was still laughing. Carried home?

"'Tis a good thing Katie has gone ta Skye ta tend her cousin Andrew or she would'a had ya by the ear for sure," continued Morna. Maitiú was still laughing.

"I be so sorry Morna, I do nay know what happened. I do nay remember any of this."

"I be tellin ya what happened, ya got into Maitiú's whiskey and the next thing we knew, you, Philip and Maitiú were dancin' jigs and singin' songs. Sara closed the tavern for ya. Ya might want to be thankin' her for that."

Maureen turned to Sara and she was chuckling as well. "I be so sorry Sara, I be makin' amends to ya."

"'Tis all right, all in all, 'twas quite entertaining," she said as she struggled to contain her laughter.

Maureen did not know what to do. She did not know what to say. She was completely humiliated in front of her friends and Maitiú was still laughing.

Akira and Braden entered the tavern and as soon as Braden saw her, he shouted, "Maitiú, Maureen's here. Hide the whiskey." Everyone started to laugh.

"That be enough, I do nay care to hear anymore! I be takin' Olaf for a ride and I will nay be back until this eve for work." Maureen grumbled

"Oh, now do nay go off mad, we just be havin' a bit of fun with ya," chuckled Elena.

"I not be havin' any fun," Maureen snapped. "I have nay had fun since I got up this day!"

"Where are ya goin'?" asked Maitiú.

41

"I do nay know for certain. I just be goin' to take Olaf and ride."

"Just be sure ya stay off the moors," warned Braden. "'Tis not safe and..." Maureen headed out of the tavern and slammed the door behind her, not waiting to hear what Braden had to say.

She ran back to the stable, tears streaming down her face. When she got there, she walked up to Olaf, buried her face in his mane and started to cry. He lowered his head and gently pushed her back to where her saddle lay across the fencing.

"Aye, yer right me friend, let's just ride." She was still upset. She saddled him up and headed north away from the tavern.

It was a most beautiful spring day in the Highlands. Maureen's mind was wandering. She thought about Katie and how she missed her. How she would be disappointed in her for last night. She thought about the patrons of the tavern who would never let her forget this. She thought about how she could have done all the things she did and not remember any of it. She had just been letting Olaf roam, not paying attention to where they were going. They had only been out for about an hour or so when she realized they had wandered out on to the moors. She brought Olaf to a stop. She tried to remember, someone had said something to her at the tavern about the moors. She looked around her and the sight of the moors in spring was beautiful. The heather was in full bloom, swaying to and fro on the breeze, and a rainbow of wildflowers covered the moor. Oh well. No matter, it was time to be heading back anyway. She pulled up the reins, but Olaf would not move. Something was wrong, Olaf was hesitating and skittish. When you are around an animal for a while you know their ways, something was out there that was making him very uneasy. She backed him off and looked around; she could not see a thing.

"What be wrong boy? What da ya see?" She gave Olaf a nudge forward, but he would not have it. Then it happened, Maureen heard the low growl from the deep grasses ahead of them and Olaf bolted. He spun around and reared up; her saddle slipped and she fell. She hit the ground hard, hitting her head. She felt something warm running down the side of her face. She looked up to see Olaf standing over her. She tried too reached for the reins, then the world around her went grey and then... darkness.

Maureen had been gone from the tavern for about two hours when Olaf wandered back down the road to the Wycked Aye. Philip was on his way to the tavern when he came upon Olaf standing on the road. He took Olaf's reins and walked him back to the Wycked Aye. As he entered the tavern, he was greeted by Master Thomas and Isabelle. They exchanged greetings and he then moved on toward the bar. It was early evening and the tavern was beginning to bustle.

Chieftain Heber was away on business, but Fionnula was there, as well as Sara, and Mistress Morna. With Katie away in Skye, Philip had been at the tavern almost every day. He approached Maitiú and asked "Where be Maureen?"

"She came into the bar earlier and we all gave her bit of a hard time about last night. She left in a fluster, took her horse an' went ridin'," said Maitiú.

"Ridin'? But Olaf be outside," said Philip. "I found

him wanderin' on the road outside the tavern. I thought he had loosened his tether, so I brought him back. She's nay here then?"

Maitiú's face changed suddenly, "Nay, she's not," he said in a solemn voice. "And Olaf's alright? Come with me Philip, let us have a look at him." As the two men approached Olaf, they found Fionnula was already there. She had Olaf by the bridal and was looking straight into his eyes. She hardly noticed when Maitiú and Philip walked up beside her.

"Fionnula?" asked Maitiú quietly, not wanting to startle the woman or the horse. "What be wrong cousin?"

Fionnula turned and said, "Look at the saddle, 'tis shifted off to one side and the straps are loose. Maureen's been thrown. Harness a carriage, we must go before darkness falls. Olaf will lead us." The two men stared at her in amazement. Fionnula looked at the two men and said, "What the bloody hell are ya waitin' for, harness a carriage!" Master Thomas and Isabella were just leaving the tavern as Maitiú and Philip were hurrying toward the stable. "What be wrong lads, ya look all in a fluster?" said Thomas.

"Mistress MacLeod has come up missin', we fear she may have taken a fall from her horse. We be off to harness a carriage," yelled Philip.

"Wait," called Thomas. "Me cart is here and already hitched. Do nay bother with the carriage, I be takin' ya."

Fionnula had already tightened the saddle on Olaf. He was almost too big for her to ride. She stopped before Isabella.

"Isabella, I would be most grateful if ya would tell the others where we have gone. And find Sara, I fear we may need her when we return." Mistress Isabella nodded her head in agreement and hurried back to the tavern. Philip and Maitiú hopped in the back of Master Thomas' cart and they headed north behind Olaf and Fionnula.

"Awaken child, awaken." A soft, gentle voice called Maureen from the darkness. "Awaken Little Mary, you are alright."

Little Mary, she had not been called that since she was a child. As she struggled to open her eyes, she saw kneeling before her the most beautiful creature she had ever seen. A small woman clothed in nothing but what appeared to be armor. Beautiful pieces of spun silver encircled her upper arms and wrists. A headdress of crystals and silver adorned a head of thick, flowing, black hair. A faint glow surrounded her. Maureen tried to sit up but her head burned with pain. She looked around for Olaf, but he was not in sight. She turned back to the woman before her.

"Who are ya?" she whispered. She was not sure if she was alive or dead. "Are ya an angel? What happened?"

"You should not have wandered on to the moors at this time. It is spring and the creatures that live here are tending new young," she said. "You and your horse ventured too close to a She-wolf and her den. You are hurt, lie still."

Braden, he had tried to warn her but she was too angry to listen. That was why he wanted her to stay off the moors. It was all coming back to her now.

"Who are ya," she asked again.

"I am Shalynn of the Tuatha De' Danann. Some

know us as the Aes Sidhe," she said. "I am Fey."

Fey, one of the Little People of Ireland, the Hill Fairies; Maureen must have hit her head harder than she thought. Surely, this must be a dream.

"But the Sidhe are of Ireland, these are the Scottish Highlands. Why would the Sidhe be here?" she asked of her dream Fairie.

"First child, I am not a dream. I am very real." She had heard Maureen's thoughts.

"The Sidhe are everywhere. We follow and keep watch over the Irish who carry the magic of the Fey in their blood."

Maureen was trying to listen and make sense of all Shalynn was saying. Her head was pounding and it was hard to concentrate on Shalynn's words. Certainly, this was all a bad dream, she should never have ridden off angry. She should have stayed at the tavern. She should have listened to Braden. How was she going to get back? Olaf had run off, the sun was setting, and she was due at the tavern to work. Mistress Morna would have her head on a skewer if she did not return.

"I need to get back to the tavern. I need to find me horse," she said as she tried to raise herself up, but it was no use. She put her hand to her head and it came away covered in blood.

"You must not move, child. Your head is wounded. You are in no condition to ride. I have sent your horse, Olaf, for your friends. He will bring them soon. You must rest now."

Shalynn reached to her belt and brought forth a small flask. She offered it to Maureen that she might drink.

Maureen took the flask and hesitated, "'Tis not whiskey, is it?"

A bit of a smile crossed Shalynn's face as she said, "No child, it is not." The water was quenching. Shalynn took the flask and poured some water on Maureen's wound. She noticed, as Shalynn handed her the flask, that the palm of her giving hand was marked with what looked to be a black rose. Maureen had seen women with markings to their skin once before, they were women from the East. But she had never seen anything like this. For not only were Shalynn's hands marked, but a goodly part of her body as well. Small dots encircled her eyes like a mask. Intricate scroll work covered her back and shoulders. "There, is that better child?"

"Why do ya call me child Shalynn, ya look to be much younger than meself."

"Ah, but in my eyes you are a child." She stood and turned to look out across the moor. It was dusk now. Small pillows of mist began to form and rest gently in the hollows of the moor. The evening symphony of the earth began to play: birds, crickets, the grasses in the spring breeze. Shalynn gazed out across the beauty before her. She spread her arms and opened her hands to the wind, as if to take in the power of the earth itself. She took a long, deep breath and said, "For three hundred years of man I have walked this earth, keeping watch over the chosen Irish who inhabit these lands."

The chosen Irish? Maureen remembered her mother telling her tales as a child, stories of the Sidhe of Ireland, stories that her Gran had told her. Maureen had barely known her Gran. Her father had taken them from Skye when she was but a babe, she did not even know her Gran's full name. "If ya watch over the Irish Shalynn, why do ya come ta me, I be Scot, not Irish?"

Shalynn paused for a moment, then turned back to her and knelt before her once again.

"You are not all Scot, child. Your mother was half Irish, her mother before her was pure Irish, and one of the chosen; you are the last of her bloodline. I bring to you a message from your mother, Maire McCrimmon MacLeod."

Maureen stared at her in disbelief, for surely her mother was in the hands of God and only able to speak with him.

"A message? But she is gone, she passed from this world many years back. She is with God."

"Passed from your world, but not from mine," Shalynn continued. "She sends a warning Little Mary, beware of the man called Robert MacLeod, the one who sired you. He brings with him nothing but pain and heartache. Heed this warning child. Should he ever return do not go to him for he will bring you harm and misfortune," she looked around and seemed a bit uneasy. "I must go soon for your friends approach to take you to safety."

"'Twas it yer magic that brought me here Shalynn?" Maureen asked.

"No child, your anger brought you here and the she-wolf in the grasses caused your horse to throw you to the ground. I would have sought you out eventually, but as you were in need, the time seemed right." She knelt close and placed her giving hand on the back of Maureen's neck to help her rest her head. Maureen felt a burning sensation and suddenly felt very tired.

"Will I ever see ya again, Shalynn?" she asked for she was falling asleep.

"I cannot say," she replied. "Remember child, the Sidhe that watch over the chosen of the Wycked Aye are true of heart and purpose. Trust in the good souls of those who surround you now, they will keep you safe. And one more thing child, do not drink any more of the Irishman's whiskey." She rose and looked south across the moor.

"Your friends are near, you are safe. Remember your mother's warning...now sleep". A bright light rose around her and then she was gone.

Fionnula had let Olaf lead the way back out on to the moors. They were not far away when a bright flash of light appeared. Fionnula turned Olaf and headed directly for it. Shalynn's departure led them straight to Maureen. When they arrived they found her peacefully sleeping. Fionnula was by her side when Philip, Maitiú and Thomas arrived with the cart. When Maitiú saw her sleeping on the ground he gasped, "Dear God is she...?"

No Maitiú," replied Fionnula. "She just be sleepin'. She has a bad wound to her head though. We must get her back to the tavern, to Sara. She be knowin' what ta do."

Maitiú lowered his head and said, "This is all me fault. I swear to ya Philip, I have done more penance as the result of the MacLeod women than I have done in me whole life." Philip and Thomas just smiled.

Sara was waiting with Isabella when they arrived back at the tavern. Sara had great skill with herbs and poultices. She could mend and heal wounds better than any court surgeon.

"Bring her to the back of the tavern" said Sara. "We have a place ready."

Sarah and Isabella cleaned and closed the wound on Maureen's head. Maureen kept dreaming of Shalynn, hearing her words of her mother's warning. As the two women worked, Sara had Isabella lift Maureen's hair to place a cool towel to the back of her neck. When she lifted the hair away, she said to Sara, "Have a look at this will ya. What do ya make of that?" Sara looked at the back of Maureen's neck and just below her hairline was a small, black rose.

By morning Maureen had regained her strength and was able to return to her chamber. Sara had done a good job mending the wound on her head. She was sore from head to toe from her fall and she still had a bit of a headache, but at least this time it was not due to Irish whiskey. Tomorrow was the Sabbath and she knew where she would be spending most of her day. She would certainly be spending some time doing penance for this whole ordeal.

It was the Sabbath morning and Maureen awoke feeling fairly well for all that she had been through. She fixed a bit of broth and bread for breakfast. She dressed in her best skirts and bodice. It was not long before there was a knock on her door. She opened it to find Maitiú.

"Good Morrow, Maureen. Peace be with you."
"And with you." she replied. He reached out and handed her a string of rosary beads. She smiled, closed the door behind them and together they walked arm in arm to confession.

Chapter Four

A Glimpse of Royalty

Photograph from Englishhistory.net

The beginning of what seemed to be a perfectly normal day had started as most do in the Highlands; with the chores of their daily lives that kept their homes warm and their bellies from growling. Maureen's was no different from most of her station, if you could even rightly say she held a station. She was truly grateful that the Chieftain had allowed her to stay at the tavern considering the trouble she had brought with her.

Her father had not been seen or heard from for many years. Many had presumed him to be dead. Katie was sure of it, and Philip had told Maureen more than once to let go of thinking that he would ever come back.

Philip would say, "Let it be girl, the man was a rogue. Aye and for sure by now he has met his end at the tip of another's sword."

Maybe he was right. But no news of such had ever

made its way to Maureen or her mother. No one had ever sent any missive of his condition good or bad. It did indeed put her situation in a bit of a jumble, for unbetroth to any man and without blood family, she would be labeled a broken woman. It would leave her with no connections, no family—an outcast. She worked hard at the tavern to earn her keep and stay in good graces of Chieftain Heber and Mistress Morna. Heber truly had no obligation to see to her wellbeing. Should he choose, he could cast her out on her ear anytime he damn well pleased. But Heber was a kind and goodly man, and she was not the only orphan to reside under the roof of the Wycked Aye. Had it not been for Heber McPherson, she would still be roaming the lowlands, scrounging for work as a serving wench and sleeping on tavern floors. Though her place in life was one of a working girl, it was not one of servitude. It was now one of proper employ.

Now mind you, that little chest of gold and jewels Maureen's father had stashed away so long ago had made things a bit more comfortable for her and quite profitable for the tavern. Heber had taken charge of the gold and jewels, and divided it for safe keeping between himself and Lord Cullen Elliot. Heber decided it would be best to keep the bounty separated and secret. That way no one could find the entire stash in one place or tie any of them to it. Part was sent to Castle Elliot and the rest was held in Heber's private keep at the tavern. No one other than Cullen, Heber and Maureen knew of it, not even Katie. Maureen still worked at the tavern as always, as the gold was basically Heber's to manage. He saw to Maureen's needs and she now had a wee cottage to live in instead of her chamber off the stables. He saw to a new saddle for Olaf, after her episode out on the moors, but other than that not much had really changed. She still cleaned the stables and fed the horses in the morning and worked at the tavern in the evening. This was her life now: the Wycked Aye Tavern was her home and these people were her family.

She little thought that Heber truly had any hope of finding a match for her. She had been on her own for a long time. She was not of a mind to get too close to any man; they were not to be trusted. They had done nothing but hurt her in the past and she bore a reputation for hurting them back. Old Ian Armstrong's face would be proof of that. Maybe there was more of her father in her than she cared to own to. She was near twenty years now and had resolved herself to this place in life. She was, in a word, happy.

Heber's cousin, Meg MacPherson, had recently arrived from Badenoch to help at the tavern. She would come to the Highland border once or twice a year to bring news of Clan Chattan to Heber and to spend time with him and her cousin, Elena. Meg was a gentle and robust woman. She had long auburn hair that she kept in a long braid and hazel-green eyes.

Katie had returned to the shire just after the Solstice. Her cousin, Andrew, had recovered enough to be on his own and she was able to return home to Philip. It was good to have her back at the tavern. Philip told her all that had happened while she had been away and she quickly took the first opening to give Maureen a sound lecture on the evils of Irish whiskey. When she had finished, Maureen did her best not to laugh, but a smirk and a smile crossed Maureen's face.

Katie's hands went immediately to her hips as she said, "And just what be so bloody funny?"

"Good to have ya home cousin" Maureen replied as she fell into full out laughter.

"Damn you girl" Katie said as she too began to laugh. Philip just shook his head and said, "God help us, the MacLeods are back together again."

It had indeed turned out to be a beautiful day in the shire. The sun was bright and the land was in full bloom in all its seasonal glory. The Highlands of Scotland were indeed something to behold in the spring and summer months. The moors were turned into rolling waves of white, lavender and purple heather as far as the eye could see. Maureen could recall her mother saying that God truly only took two days to make most of the world and spent the rest of his time on Scotland. It was always comforting to Maureen to see the earth and all her creatures start anew with the change of the seasons.

Mistress Morna had sent her off to the apothecary for a few supplies for the tavern. Sara had joined her as she too was in need of herbs and medicinals. As they walked, they passed by the little rectory next to the Catholic Chapel where Father Brian Desmond resided. He was outside tending the parish grounds.

"Good Marrow to ya Mistress MacLeod, I have missed ya at Mass on Sunday. Ya need nay be in the company of an Irishman to come to Mass, don't ya know."

"Aye, Father that I know," Maureen replied. "I be seein' ya real soon."

Sarah said, "I noticed that ya have nay been goin' to Mass since Maitiú left for Ireland."

"Nay, I have not. I do nay feel safe goin' by meself" she sighed. "There be so few left now in the shire that celebrate the Mass. Most have gone the way of Luther and are none too happy with those of us who still hold to the Mother Church. I can feel the town men watchin' me when I walk to Mass, I do nay like it."

"Times are changin' for sure," said Sara. "I little think there be much we can do but to wait and see if it turns out for the better."

They turned the corner on the lane and entered the apothecary of Master Liam McGuire. Maureen loved going into Master Liam's shop. There were so many wonderful things to catch the eye: oils, soaps, spices, herbs. It was always an adventure for the senses. Master Liam greeted them with a rousing, "Good Marrow Mistresses, how fair thee this day?"

"Well, indeed Master Liam. I have a list from Mistress Morna at the tavern. Can ya fill it fer me?" Maureen asked.

"Aye, anything for the Tánaiste. Give us the list lass, will nay take a moment." And with that he disappeared to the back of the shop. Sara was occupied with the selection of various dried herbs and tinctures when a messenger entered the establishment. But this was not just any messenger, this was a royal messenger.

Sara and Maureen both startled as he barked, "Shopkeeper, pray heed, come forth!" Master Liam came rushing at the call of this pompous peacock of a herald.

"Be ye the proprietor of this establishment?" questioned the messenger. "Aye Sir, that I am. Master Liam McGuire at Her Majesty's service," he replied.

"Be it known that Her Majesty, Mary Regina Stuart, will arrive at this shire in five days' time on progress through her kingdom. Her Majesty shall be holding open court to hear counsel of the Highland nobility and meet her people. See this message is spread." And with that he turned and departed to the next merchant down the lane.

The three of them just stared at each other until Master Liam broke an enormous smile across his face and exclaimed, "Bloody hell, the Queen's comin'."

Word spread like wildfire through the shire of the arrival of the Queen. Her Majesty and her Court had passed this way before on her travels to Edinburg. The main roads were not that far from the Highland shire, but to have her stop there was quite an event indeed. By the time Sara and Maureen returned to the tavern, everyone already knew.

People from miles around would be coming this way to get a glimpse of Her Majesty and to bring their wares to trade and sell. Merchants and crafters of all sorts would be preceding the Queen with their wagons and tents to line the streets for a Marketer's Faire. A grand time it would be indeed.

It would also be a very busy and dangerous time for the tavern. For not only would the peasant folk be filling the shire, but the surrounding nobles as well. The noblemen of the Highlands and neighboring Lowlands would be arriving to seek audience with Her Majesty; and with them would come their entourage of servants, advisors and guardsmen... and with them, came the spies and the thieves.

The return of Mary Stuart to the throne did not please all of the people of Scotland. The Protestants and Calvinists were wary of the young Queen. For Mary Stuart was Roman Catholic and with her return to Scotland many feared the return of the Papacy. "God's anointed Queen" they called her. She was a threat; a threat to the Protestants, a threat to the Calvinists and most of all, a threat to her cousin, Queen Elizabeth I of England.

When word first reached the tavern of the Queen's intended arrival, Chieftain Heber immediately sent urgent missives to the men of the Highlands whose loyalty lie with the Chieftain, and who he could depend on to come to the Wycked Aye to help protect him, his alliances and his tavern.

Mistress Morna had been going over the pantry viands for the tavern when she called to Heber.

"Chieftain, the pantry has nay enough on hand to manage the Queen's arrival. We be needin' lamb and venison, and at least ten grouse. Ya need to send Grady out huntin' and we be needin' to slaughter one of the spring lambs." Heber seemed not to be listening as he walked toward the bar and his frantic Tánaiste.

"Heber...Heber, where be yer mind man? Have ya nay heard a word I be sayin'?"

"Settle yerself woman, I be hearin' every damn word," he replied. He stepped around the bar and turned his back to the patrons of the tavern to have a discrete conversation with his Tánaiste.

"Now ya know Morna, we two have been through this before at the tavern and ya know what we be in fer." Morna simply nodded in agreement.

"I want ya to make sure that all the girls, and Grady, are carryin' blades from now until I say different. We should have plenty of protection if me missives are received in time. Hopefully, we be gettin' through this without the place bein' torn apart."

"I be seein' to it, Heber," replied Morna. She placed her hand on Heber's arm and said, "I be warnin' the lasses."

Heber placed his hand upon hers and said, "Aye, I be sendin' the hunters out for ya Morna, and we be gettin' yer pantry filled in no time. Oh, and Maitiú should be arrivin' any day with our shipment of Desmond ale."

Within a day familiar faces began to arrive. Akira and Braden Elliot were welcomed with open arms. Lord Cullen and Lady Gwendolyn Elliot were the next to arrive. Philip, Connor, Grady and Master Thomas were all present and accounted for. As the Chieftain called his men together, Mistress Morna called her girls together as well.

Morna MacGregor was a hard-working woman. She had been brought to the Wycked Aye by her sister, Dame Brittah Sutherland H'elie, the owner of the tavern. Morna had no husband and so she devoted herself to the Wycked Aye Tavern. Although she was a petite woman, she controlled the tavern with a firm hand. But beneath that commanding exterior was a kind woman with a heart of gold who truly cared about the tavern and her girls that worked there.

"Now some of ya already know what be happinin' here in the next few days" Morna began.

"Elena, you, Sara and Katie have been with us for such occasions before so you be knowin' what to expect." They nodded in agreement.

"For the rest of ya, we be workin' straight through so just be ready for it. Chieftain also wants each of ya to be carryin' a blade or dagger while the tavern is full of..."

"But Tánaiste," Maureen interrupted. "Chieftain da' nay allow anyone to carry weapons in the tavern and..."

"Aye, Maureen, that be true. But this be different. 'Tis fer yer own safety, so mind yerself well and do nay act in haste." She looked straight at Maureen, "and keep that doe-hoofed dagger of yers well covered." They all just looked at each other, not really knowing what to expect. Isabella, Detta and Maureen exchanged a worried glance. Mistress Morna saw the looks of apprehension on their faces and said, "'Tis only for a day or two, we just bein' careful. Now lasses, off to yer duties." And with that she dismissed them to attend to their usual chores.

As Maureen began to move through the tavern preparing for the evening festivities, she noticed the men were still at the Chieftain's table and their meeting was far more serious than theirs.

"As I was sayin' lads, the Queen's Halberdiers will be in full complement to guard Her Majesty. But I want ya to be mindful of any talk or actions that might be of concern to Her Majesty's safety," warned Heber.

"I have word that Armstrong be on his way along with a few strong arms. I know not their purpose, but they be headed this way," said Cullen.

The Chieftain continued, "Well, there ya have it, keep yer wits about ya lads. Any information goes straight to Sir Teague and Captain Sommerville. Ya know as well as I do that there be many who be none too happy with our young Queen. But this tavern remains loyal to the Crown—eyes and ears open lads, understood?" The men all nodded their heads in agreement.

Maitiú had tried to explain the complexities of the politics of the Scottish Clans to Maureen one night in the tavern. His dealings for the Earl of Desmond had taken him all over Scotland and the Isles, and he knew the Clans well. It was all so mashed and mingled together; clans fighting with each other over land, cattle, money and faith. Alliances seemed to change with the new moon. It was getting to the point where you could not trust anyone.

It was the day before the Queen's arrival and the shire was buzzing like a hornet's nest. The hunters had been successful and the pantry had twelve fine grouse and fresh venison as well. Maureen had only one more grouse to pick, clean, and put up for roasting when Morna came into the pantry.

"Good God girl, yer up to yer elbows in grouse innards. Do nay be throwin' any of that away now, we be usin' it in the stews," she said.

"Aye Mistress, I know. I put them all aside and salted them down. And the venison be butchered and packed as well."

"Why do ya nay take some time and go out to the marketer's faire Maureen. Ya have nay left the tavern since all the festivities began. There be so much to see, all the nobles prancin' around and all the wares to look over. A girl can always use a new skirt and bodice." She winked at her and smiled.

"Are ya sure 'twould be alright?"

"Aye, most certainly. Katie be out front and I be sure it would nay take much to get her to go along.

Now go rinse all those bird entrails off yer arms, and go have a wee bit of fun." Maureen started to give her a hug when Morna put her hands up and said, "Wash first, then hug."

Katie was so excited she could hardly be contained. She loved the glamour surrounding the ladies of Court and the noble women. She loved looking at their beautiful gowns and assorted adornments. She loved all the drama of nobility and the conversations of Court. Maureen cared not for the gossip mongering and carrying favor that goes on at Court. She belonged with simple folk, the salt of earth her mother used to say.

"I can hardly wait for you to see cousin. There be silks, and woolens, and linens, and beautiful threads for our embroidery. We can even get ya a nice piece of white linen for a Sabbath apron." God love her, Maureen had told Katie that she did not need a Sabbath apron, but Katie insisted. Maureen did not understand the need for an apron you could not wipe your hands on.

She continued, "There are leather craftsmen, and iron workers and jewelers and..."

Maureen stopped her at that, "Jewelers, be there a silversmith? Did ya see any silver crosses Katie?" she asked. Katie looked at her curiously and said, "Aye, but they be costly cousin, made for the purse of a noble."

"Could ya show me please, 'tis important," Maureen asked. They meandered through the street, stopping here and there to look at all the crafts and wares. Maureen spotted a lovely bodice at Mistress Bree's that would do quite nicely for Mass on Sundays, and only two farthings. It fit nicely and Katie said it did her well.

There was so much to see, it was truly quite a festival indeed. They approached the silversmith and as Katie had said, this was a place for the heavy purses of the nobles and not the satchel of a peasant girl. Fancy skirts and velvet doublets filled this part of the market. The nobles looked at them as if they were on an errand for their own noble ladies for surely, they had no business there on their own.

"Beg pardon Master Smith, would ya have any small Irish crosses in the old Gaelic style?" Maureen asked. The silversmith rolled his eyes at her as if she was completely wasting his time and pointed her to the other end of the table. She looked to the end of table where an older nobleman stood, admiring the wares.

As she and Katie moved next to the Gentleman, Katie asked, "What do ya need a silver cross fer Maureen?"

"Tis not fer me Katie, it be a gift."

"A silver, Gaelic cross...a gift? Do nay tell me yer spendin' yer hard-earned silver on that bogmouse, Maitiú," she said as her hands went to her hips in a motherly stance that clearly said, I do not approve.

"Well, that be me idea and please cousin, do nay be callin' him a bogmouse. Ya know times have been hard for Maitiú lately, maybe this would lift his spirits and bring him a bit of luck as well."

She found a beautiful cross in the old style with a Celtic circle in the middle. But as they expected, the Smith wanted four pence for it. As she let out a sigh of disappointment, the noble gentleman next to them turned and spoke in a beautiful French accent.

"I do beg your pardon Mistresses, but I could not help but overhear your conversation. Allow me to introduce myself. My name is Francois." Katie and Maureen both bowed respectfully to this kind French gentleman. "I believe I am acquainted with this Irishman you speak of. Maitiú MacRoibeard de Faoite, is it not?"

"I M'lord." Maureen could not believe her ears. How could this Frenchman know Maitiú?

"It sorrows me to hear of his misfortune. Messier de Faoite has been of service to me and someone very close to me in the past. Please Mistress, allow me." With that he called the silversmith over and began to pay for the cross.

"Nay M'lord, I can nay accept such a generous..." he raised his hand to stop her. Maureen did not argue. "'Tis most kind indeed. May God bless ya M'lord," she said.

"Merci, mademoiselle. Please give my respects to Messier de Faoite," then he took her hand, gently placed a kiss to it and bid them good day. The silversmith placed the Gaelic cross in a little velvet bag and handed it to Maureen. She looked at the velvet bag and then at Katie. Maureen was speechless. Finally, she said, "Katie, what the hell just happened?"

Katie shook her head and said, "I do nay bloody know."

They began their trip back to the tavern, working their way through the crowded lanes. As Maureen moved through the crowd, she began to have a feeling that they were being watched. She kept turning around to look behind her to see who was following, but no one was there.

"Maureen, what be wrong girl?" Katie could tell that she was uneasy.

"Oh, I can nay be sure, 'tis nothin' cousin, I just feel like someone be watchin' us."

Katie stopped walking and took a glance around. When she looked back, she saw two men following behind who stopped abruptly and turned their backs to her. She did not share this with Maureen, she just said, "I do nay see anything lass. Come on, we best be getting' back to the tavern."

The Queen would be arriving on the morrow, and the tavern would be very busy this night.

They needed to get back to the tavern. As they walked, they passed by the alleyway that led to the Chapel. Maureen stopped and looked at the velvet bag, "Katie, would ya mind if I stopped at Chapel? I be catchin' up with ya in just a bit. Tell Morna I be on me way."

"Of course, cousin, give me best to Father Desmond" she replied. She headed on back up the lane to the tavern. Maureen entered the Chapel, crossed herself with Holy water and went in search of Father Desmond. The Chapel was so peaceful in the late of the day. She found him on the commoner's side of the altar placing new candles on the table in front of the prayer bench.

"Good marrow, Father. Peace be with you."

"Well, well, Maureen, what brings ya here at such an hour? 'Tis almost three of the clock. I surely do nay have time to hear your confession this day," he said with a little smile on his face. She found that humorous in a way and a bit disheartening in another.

"I have nay come for confession Father. I have a wee bit of a favor to ask. I have a silver cross here and I would like to give it to a friend, could ya bless it fer me Father?" He took the velvet bag and withdrew the Gaelic cross.

"Ah, what a lovely cross, in the old tradition. From the looks of this, I believe we be needin' an Irish blessin'."

"Aye Father that we do, one fer happiness and good fortune."

The tavern was full to the brim as expected. It was quite an exciting night to be sure. There was a constant flow of nobles and Clan leaders making their way to Heber's table throughout the night. Maureen was truly impressed at how many men of high rank waited to seek counsel with their Chieftain. Elena would point out this person and that person, and she greatly enjoyed giving all the scuttlebutt on each and every one.

Just past dark the door opened and in walked three of the Queen's Halberdiers: Captain Duncan Sommerville, Captain Craig Melville and Sir Teague Seaton. On the arm of Sir Teague walked a most beautiful Irish woman. She wore a leather bog dress and was fully armed. She walked with the poise of a noble woman, but also with the strength and confidence of a skilled warrior. She was not pleased when she was asked to remove her weapons and place them in the weapons rack. Sir Teague reassured her it would be alright and she reluctantly removed them. Maureen was quite sure that, in truth, she was not fully disarmed at all...just like her. Maureen hurried over to Elena for she would know who this lady was for certain.

"Elena, who be that woman with the guardsmen?" Maureen asked.

"That be Sir Teague's new bride, Cailín Rua Kelly Seaton. She be an Irish Mercenary, been on more campaigns than you can count, until she met up with Sir Teague. Now she travels with the Queen and the Guard," Elena whispered.

Maureen was fascinated with this woman.

"But how could such a lovely thing as that be a warrior and a mercenary?" she asked.

"Aye, she has the face of an angel with the heart of a lioness," replied Elena. "Word be she be a master swordsman and not one to be trifled with."

They had been seated at their table for only a short while when Sir Teague called Mistress Morna to them and requested an audience with Chieftain Heber. Morna conveyed the message to Heber and it was not long before they were called to the Chieftain's table. Ale, cheese and fruit were requested at his table as the meeting with Her Majesty's Guardsmen and Lady Seaton continued for some time. There was no clinking of tankards and no laughter coming from this meeting. Something was afoot and it appeared to be of a most serious nature.

Maureen brought the tray of food and an extra pitcher of ale. When she reached the table, all conversation stopped. She filled everyone's tankards and was immediately dismissed by Chieftain Heber.

As Morna had warned them, they would be working through the night and so it was that the last of the patrons did not take leave of the Wycked Aye until near two of the clock in the wee hours of the morning. Everyone was completely exhausted. Tomorrow the Queen would arrive in their little shire and these simple folks would be treated to a small glimpse of royalty. All Maureen wanted was a bite of food, a warm bed and two new feet.

It was just after dawn and the lanes of the shire were already beginning to bustle. Goodly folk of all walks were arriving to partake of the festivities and to see Her Majesty, Mary Regina Stuart. A large tent of sorts had been raised for the Queen and was completely surrounded by Royal Guardsmen. Maureen very much wanted to stay and watch the progress of Her Majesty, but stables still needed to be cleaned and horses needed to be fed. She watched the spectacle for a few more minutes and then turned and headed back up to the stables. As she came up the lane, walking towards her was Lady Cailín Seaton. She stepped aside and bowed properly saying, "Good Marrow, M'lady."

Lady Seaton continued for a few steps and then turned saying, "Beg pardon Mistress, ya seem familiar."

"I be Maureen MacLeod M'lady," she obediently replied. "I served yer table last eve at the Wycked Aye. May I be of service?"

She cocked her head slightly and stepped back toward her. "Maureen MacLeod, would ya be of relation to one Robert MacLeod?" she asked as she raised her chin just slightly.

"Aye, M'lady," Maureen replied cautiously. "He would be me Father, but I have nay seen him for many, many years. Do ya have word of his condition?" Maureen truly feared the answer to this question, but she had to ask. As Philip often told her, her mouth tends to goes off before her brain can do anything about it.

"Me last contact with him be over three years back on campaign just over the border in England," she replied. "I know not of his current condition. Unfortunately, Mistress, our loyalties be in different directions." And with that she turned and began to walk away.

"M'lady?" Maureen followed after her and Lady Seaton turned to face her. "I'd be most grateful for anything ya could tell me of him."

She drew a deep breath contemplating her response and replied, "I be afraid Mistress that what I recall of Robert MacLeod would nay be worth the tellin', especially to his daughter. Good day."

The look on her face said far more than her words. It was the same look that covered Maureen's face when she thought of that toad Armstrong, pure hatred. Disheartened and suddenly feeling very alone, Maureen walked back to the stables.

Cailín continued down the lane toward the Queen's Pavilion. Her husband had arrived much earlier and was already standing guard with the rest of the Halberdiers.

She continued down the lane for a short distance, then turned to make sure young Mistress MacLeod was no longer in sight. She pulled her cloak around her and pulled her hood over her head, for she too had an assignment for Her Majesty. Today she would be the spy.

She headed toward the Marketer's Faire and then toward the outskirts of the shire. She wandered through the market pretending to admire the wares as she scanned the faces in the crowd for the two men she was sent to find. The first was Ian Armstrong, a Lowlander and head of Clan Armstrong. He was a gallowglass, a border reiver and suspected traitor to Scotland. The second was James Hepburn, Fifth Earl of Bothwell and Lord High Sheriff of Scotland. This man's loyalties and intentions were always in question.

As she moved through the shire, she caught sight of her first target, Armstrong. He was walking away from the faire, heading toward the edge of the shire. She turned to follow.

He walked on, past the inn and then down an alleyway next to the blacksmith. Cailín hurried past the blacksmith and slipped around the back of the building near the horse stalls. She knelt down behind some bushes and watched as Armstrong approached a carriage. Leaning against the back of the carriage was Hepburn. The two men spoke briefly, then Hepburn handed Armstrong a pouch. Clearly it was payment, for what she could not know. She had seen all she needed to see. She must hurry back now to meet with Sir Teague and Chieftain Heber. She watched as the meeting between the amadans ended. As Hepburn got into his carriage, his coachman snapped the reins and the horses jolted into motion.

As the carriage pulled away, a third man appeared from behind. A man she had not planned on seeing, a man she knew to be dangerous. A man she had hated for a very long time.

By mid-morning the stables were clean. Maureen was giving Olaf his usual carrot when Katie and Philip came hurrying in.

"Come on cousin, you must see. The Queen has arrived. Hurry now, before ya miss it." Before Maureen could respond Katie grabbed her and dragged her out of the stables. As they approached, they could see a great procession of pipers, drummers and flag bearers. The Queen's Guard led the way followed by Her Majesty, Mary Stuart and then her ladies in waiting. A young and pretty thing she was indeed, only nineteen years and the ruler of Scotland, so young to carry such a burden.

All of the noble women were dressed in beautiful, ornate gowns, a sign of their station as wards of the Court. It was quite a sight to see. The Queen's Courtiers followed behind tossing hard candies and small trinkets to the children in the crowd who laughed and giggled at the excitement. The procession moved on toward the tent where Her Majesty would meet with Highland nobles and clan leaders. Katie and Maureen stayed away from the procession, as Maureen was dirty from cleaning the stables and not presentable for such an occasion. Philip had gone ahead and was moving around through the crowd, as he was known to many of the clan leaders and had recited his poetry for them on his travels through Scotland. Katie watched proudly as her man was recognized and greeted by many of higher station.

Once the Queen was seated on her dais, open court began. There, waiting with many others to speak with Her Majesty, stood Chieftain Heber, Captain Duncan Sommerville and Sir & Lady Seaton. Maureen turned to Katie, pointing in the direction of the Chieftain and asked, "Katie look, what be goin' on there? Their meeting last night at the tavern and now they go together to see the Queen?"

Katie looked toward the Chieftain and said, "I do nay know, cousin. I just do nay know. Let me speak with Philip and see what I can find out."

Maureen's time for play had come to an end. The tavern would be filling very soon as patrons stopped by for one last ale. Katie joined Philip and they continued to mingle with the crowd. Maureen returned home to clean up and then to the tavern and to work.

As she entered the tavern, Mistress Morna and Lady Gwen were seated at Chieftain's table. Lord Cullen was at Court, as was Master Thomas and Isabella, Sara and Elena. Only a few patrons sat here and there nibbling on breads and cheese.

"Have ya had any word of Maitiú' M'lady?" Morna asked of Gwen.

"He was due back from Ireland almost two days ago with a new shipment of ale for the tavern. I must say, I be a bit concerned over our Irish bogtrotter."

Gwen looked at Morna with surprise for the Tánaiste did not voice her concerns about anyone too often. Morna MacGregor was a hard-working woman. She was here as Tánaiste to the Chieftain and to run a tavern and that is exactly what she did. If Morna was beginning to worry then maybe there was good reason to do so.

Gwen put a smile on her face and said, "Oh do nay worry over Maitiú'. He and Maire will be here soon enough. I be quite certain that all be well and they just be a bit delayed."

Maureen did not interject in the conversation. Maitiú had been in Ireland for some time now. The Desmond brewery was not doing as well as it had in the past. Times were becoming hard for everyone. They had expected Maitiú and his daughter, Maire, to arrive before the Queen, but there had been no sign of him and no word.

Maureen did not realize that she had stopped what she was doing and was staring blankly at both of the women, listening to their conversation.

"Have ya no work to do?" Morna said as she brought Maureen back to the moment.

"Beg pardon Tánaiste, 'tis not me place," and she quickly went off about her chores.

The Queen and her Court had left their little shire and moved on to Edinburg. Almost everyone had returned to the tavern after Court had concluded. Cullen and Gwen had left early and returned to their rooms at the inn just down the lane. It was a rousing night at the tavern. Many of the Queens Guard were enjoying their time to the fullest. Laughter, stories, poetry, dancing and song; all were in fine spirits for sure, and all that singing and dancing made these people hungry and thirsty.

Maureen was at the back of the tavern pulling lamb off the fire when she saw them enter the tavern. She thought to herself, Oh no, dear God no. Every bit of breath left her.

Shoulder to shoulder they walked, it seemed as if their motion had slowed and every sound, every movement was amplified. The blaggards looked like wolves surrounding an innocent and unsuspecting flock. The first two were very familiar. They had come to the tavern before looking for her on orders from that filthy toad of a Lowlander. Behind them walked the toad himself, Armstrong. Every time she saw that scar across his face it gave her a wee bit of satisfaction. If she could, she would run him through herself. But the sting of her doe-hoofed dagger was but a tiny victory compared to the pain and disgrace this man had given to her. May the good Lord forgive her, but she hated him.

Heber had seen them enter as well, Maureen's glance darted to him and his to hers. What she saw in her Chieftain's eyes was the look of an alert warrior and she felt a sense of urgency in his gaze. She knew that in her eyes he saw nothing but pure fear. Although none of the patrons really noticed, the feel of the tavern gradually became tense as the family of the Wycked Aye realized who had just entered. Though she herself had not confided all of the circumstances of this situation to them, every one of them knew this was trouble. Most of them had been present when Heber threw them out of the tavern and warned them never to return.

The Chieftain, Braden and Connor moved quickly to confront their path. Maureen turned her face away and her back to the door. She was frozen in place, afraid to move for fear of bringing attention to herself. Before she knew what was happening, Philip had his arm around her waist and was shuffling her out of sight.

"Philip, what the hell are ya..."

"Sssh!" he snapped. "Fer once in yer life can ya just be quiet!" He whisked her off to the back of the pantry behind the ale kegs. "Now stay here out of sight until this be finished." And with that he returned to the main hall of the tavern.

Heber confronted Armstrong in the middle of the tavern hall with Braden and Connor at his side.

"Well, Master Armstrong, 'twould appear that I was not completely clear about yer patronage to me tavern. Allow me to clear that up. Ya be not welcome here, now be on yer way."

"Chieftain MacPherson, now what kind of a greetin' be that now? Aye and for sure 'tis not the reputation of the Wycked Aye to turn away a thirsty traveler," he snidely replied.

Heber glanced around the tavern taking an account of the patrons filling his establishment. There were common folk and families with little ones on holiday to the faire. There were merchants, a few country gentlemen and two tables of the Queen's Guardsmen. This was not the time for a confrontation and Heber knew it.

"If thirsty be all that ya be, then take yer rabble ta the bar and fill their cups. Then off with ya. There be nothing more for ya here." Armstrong simply nodded in agreement and Braden and Connor moved aside to allow the blaggards to pass. As they passed by, Armstrong's men purposely bumped shoulders with Connor and Braden. That brought the attention of the Guardsmen who rose from their tables and began to tactically maneuver through the tavern. As Armstrong passed, he turned to the Chieftain.

"Oh, and by the way Heber, ya do have somethin' fer me here. Ya can nay hide that little green-eyed wildcat forever. She be not yer charge. She be payin' me what she owes me—one way or another." He turned his back to the Chieftain and walked toward the bar. Chieftain's eyes narrowed and his jaw tensed. The anger rolling off of Heber was like thunder, but he made no move. The men went to the bar where Elena reluctantly filled their cups.

One of the men said, "Here be to ya, lass."

Elena replied, "Blow it out yer hole."

Maureen had not heard any of the confrontation herself. She was alone in the back of tavern, knelt down between the ale kegs when she heard a faint voice whisper in her ear.

"Run child, run now, run for your life." Shalynn. Maureen was not of a mind to disregard her warning. She moved far enough back around to catch the attention of Elena and signaled to her that she was leaving. Elena gave her a quick tilt of her head that told her to go. Maureen grabbed her basket and slipped out the back of the tavern, quietly hurrying through the darkness to the safety of her little cottage.

The Guardsmen had moved up to the bar and made it very clear that Armstrong and his men would be better off having an ale elsewhere. The toad and his boys finished their tankards and peacefully left. It did not take long for the patrons to return to their usual laughter and song, which played on well into the night.

It was near midnight and all of the lasses of the tavern were completely exhausted. The pantry was close to empty and the ale barrels were running dry. There were still a few stragglers left at the tavern enjoying what was left of the ale.

Philip was behind the bar when a large man, ragged from travel approached the bar and requested an ale and a whiskey. This man was road weary, dirty and battle scarred. He smelled of horse sweat and

Philip noticed that the knuckles of his right hand were stained with blood.

"Good Marrow," Philip said cautiously. "Looks as if ya been on the move for some time. There be a fine Inn just up the way and..."

"Will nay be needin' an inn barkeep. I have some business to attend to and then I be movin on," he grumbled.

"Well then, welcome to the Wycked Aye. What be yer name good Sir?" asked Philip.

The man took another swig of ale, wiped his mouth with his shirt sleeve and replied, "The name be MacLeod, Robert MacLeod."

Maureen scurried across the lane and up the hill to her little cottage. She had come this way so many times after the tavern had closed it was not difficult to find her way in the dark of night. She entered her cottage and quietly bolted the door behind her. As she turned away from the door, she noticed that one of her shutters was ajar. Panic gripped her and she could not move. It took her a moment to regain herself and muster the courage to look about the room. As she glanced over to her bed, she saw two sandaled feet hanging off of it, they were not moving. She said a quick prayer and crossed herself. She slowly reached under her skirt and drew her dagger from inside her boot. As she approached the bed, she realized that above the sandals were Irish trews, and above that floated the full sleeves of a léine.

"Dear God, Maitiú!" she exclaimed. But he did not respond. She quickly lit a candle and moved over to him. As the candle light reached him, she could see that his face had been badly beaten.

"Mary, Mother of God, who did this Maitiú?" He still did not respond. She placed her hands on his chest and gently tried to rouse him, "Labhair liom, a Maitiú, speak to me." He groaned and tried to open his eyes but they were too swollen, he was barely conscious.

"He be here," he said.

"Who be here Maitiú?" He was rambling and not making any sense. "Stay put Maitiú', I be goin' for help." As Maureen was reaching for her cloak, she noticed her keepsake chest on the bench. She opened the chest and took out the little velvet bag. She took the silver cross and placed it around Maitiú's neck.

"May God keep ya safe me friend." Then she ran as quickly as she could to the inn for Gwen and Cullen. She woke Cullen and he was none too happy until she explained about Maitiú. He and Gwen came immediately. She then ran back through the shire for Sara. She too was none too happy to be awakened, but she collected her medicinals and came as well.

"So, this be why he was late, what happened?" asked Gwen.

"I do nay know M'lady, all he said was, 'He be here'," Maureen replied.

"Well, where be his horses? Where be the ale wagon and..?" Gwen's face suddenly went very pale. She turned and grabbed Cullen by both forearms. "Dear God Cullen, where be Maire?"

Chapter Five

Sword of Honor

Philip MacAlisdair was no fool. He knew full well that the renegade gallowglass standing before him was a volatile and dangerous man. He also knew that this man's presence in the shire placed the tavern and everyone in it in grave danger. It was late, and only two or three patrons remained in the Wycked Aye. There was no point in drawing any attention to him now. The tavern had survived the Queen's arrival and dealt with enough confrontation for one day.

As the gallowglass finished his whiskey and ale, he placed a crown on the bar and drew a soiled shirtsleeve across his mouth. As he turned to leave the tavern, Philip cleverly issued a most polite and clear warning as to the identity of this mysterious man.

"Fare thee well then Robert MacLeod and good journey to ya Sir," Philip announced. MacLeod did not acknowledge Philip's cordialities. He simply pulled his weapons from the rack and left the tavern. As the door closed behind him, eyes glanced back and forth between the few workers left at the Wycked Aye.

Finally, when the last of the patrons had gone, Elena bolted the door behind them. The moment the latch was secure she turned to Heber.

"God's teeth Heber, what the bloody hell is he doin' here!" Before Heber could respond she turned on Philip.

"And you, ya said he was dead! I thought ya said he was dead!" she exclaimed. "This be trouble for sure brother, Armstrong and his ruffians earlier and now MacLeod. They be after her ya know and we be sittin' smack in the middle of it. What could they possibly want with her Heber; the wretch be as poor as dirt?"

Heber did not respond. He knew full well what these men were after and feared that young Mistress MacLeod would end up paying a very high price for it. Not even Heber knew the extent of the circumstances surrounding that chest of gold and jewels. But he did know that its existence and its scattered locations could never be told, not to anyone, no matter the cost. Morna, Philip and Elena gathered around Heber awaiting his bidding.

"There be not a thing we can do about it this night." The concern in Heber's voice was clear. "Where be our little green-eyed wildcat anyway?"

"I tucked her away between the ale kegs when Armstrong and his boys arrived. I have nay seen her since," said Philip.

"She left hours ago brother," Elena said softly. "She went back to her cottage, alone." Heber raised his gaze to meet Elena's.

80

"'Tis too dangerous to go after her now. They may be watchin'. She's made it through many a night alone before, pray God she gets through this one."

As the gallowglass walked from the tavern a bit of a grin crossed his face. He had made himself know, his plan was set in motion. The moon was bright this night as he made his way back toward the blacksmith. There he would meet up with Armstrong at the Irishman's ale wagon where they would make their plans for the marrow. None of this would have been needed if the Irishman had done as they asked, he thought to himself. Put up a damn good fight he did, too bad they had to leave him for dead, and too bad that little lass of his got away. Never to mind, they be not worth the worry. In the next day or so all would be set to right. He would have his chest of gold, be rid of a troublesome girl-child and be well on his way back to England.

He continued his walk through the shire amidst the quiet of the night. As he passed by the local inn, he suddenly felt uneasy. MacLeod was a skilled and seasoned warrior. His senses were keen and his eyes sharp. He slowed his pace and let his hand come to rest upon the hilt of his sword. He glanced around, seeing only the movement of rats and mice in the alleyways. Relaxing his guard, he continued on his way toward the blacksmith. Yet he knew, somewhere in the night, someone was watching.

"Come away from the window wife," Sir Teague whispered to his bride. It was late and morning would be coming soon. Lady Seaton was restless as she watched the figure of a man move through the street in the moonlight. She had seen him earlier at the meeting with Armstrong, and recognized him instantly. As she watched him walk, the anger in her heart grew and the words in her mind were clear.

"I see ya MacLeod, I see ya. And this time ya'll not be gettin' away."

Lady Gwendolyn resigned herself to her husband's arms. "Maire, my sweet Maire, where could she be Cullen?" she asked as she began to cry. Cullen wrapped his arms around his wife and laying a gentle hand to her head whispered, "Da nay worry me love, we be findin' her, I promise ya." As she raised her eyes to meet his, her tears began to subside, calmed by the strength and promise of a man she loved so dear.

"Aye, do calm yerself cousin, Maire be safe."

Startled, everyone turned toward the cot. As Maitiú' strained to raise himself from the bed, Sara placed a hand gently on his chest.

"Maitiú', I pray ya stay still. "'Tis not wise to be movin' about in yer condition. We know not where ya may be broken and…"

"Sara, yer an angel of mercy fer sure and I be most grateful for yer kindness and care, but 'tis not as bad as ya think. Believe me, 'tis been worse." As he sat up and Cullen got a better look at his face he said, "Aye, he be right, I've seen worse."

Sara handed Maitiú another cold cloth soaked in herbs. As he placed the cloth to one side of his battered face, Gwen knelt before him and asked, "Maitiú', pray where be Maire, what be goin' on cousin?"

"Well lass," Maitiú replied, "I do believe I can tell ya what happened, but I have little idea what be goin' on."

They all listened as Maitiú told of how Armstrong and his trolls had stopped the ale cart just outside of the shire on the road to the tavern. How they had threatened to take Maire unless Maitiú delivered Maureen back to them. How Maire had managed to break fee and run away.

Up until then Maureen had been sitting on a stool at her small table, staying quiet and out of the way of the noble woman and her kin. At Maitiú's words all eyes turned to her.

"But how could they know that Maitiú? How could they know of our acquaintance?" Maureen asked.

"Armstrong has had his spies keepin' an eye on ya lass. They been watchin' us walk to Mass and such. They know ya serve the Chieftain at the tavern and keep the stables." He paused for a moment, "and they know where yer cottage be."

"What do they want with me? I swear to ya, with God as me witness, I know not what be afoot here." Maureen leaned forward and placed her face in her hands. Her heart was aching, for a dear and loyal friend had taken a terrible beating on her account, without even knowing why. This was her fault, all her fault.

Maitiú continued, "They seem to be of a mind that ya be in possession of something of great value."

Maureen looked to Lord Cullen and they exchanged a brief glance.

"They told me that if I did nay bring ya and what ya owed them back, I would nay see me daughter again. That be when Maire broke away. I told her to run, to run to God. I knew she would head for the Chapel, to Father Desmond. She be in the safe keepin' of the good sisters at the convent, I be sure of it. I fought back fer as long as I could, but the odds were just a wee bit in their favor. They left me fer dead, took the ale wagon and horses and headed this way."

"So, 'twas Armstrong," Maureen whispered. "That be what ya meant when ya said he be here."

"Nay lass, nay," Maitiú grimaced a bit as he changed position. "Another man traveled with them. A man they called MacLeod, Robert MacLeod. 'Tis yer father who be back lass, and I little think he be interested in any kind of family reunion."

Maureen stared at Maitiú in disbelief. She suddenly felt very alone. To hear that her own father would toss her aside or even take her life for a bag of gold was more painful than anything Armstrong had ever done to her. She turned her face away from the others in the room. She could not face them.

The hour was late and it was Lord Cullen who now took control of the situation.

"This be grave indeed. Maitiú, stay here. They have left ya for dead and we need to keep it that way for the time bein'. We make no move this night. Sara, Lady Gwendolyn and I shall see ya back to yer cottage. Come daylight we shall seek counsel with Heber. Mistress MacLeod, go about yer chores at the stables as always and then make yer way to the safety of the tavern, and bring me wife's dear cousin with ya. Off we go now, quickly, quietly."

As the door closed behind them, Maitiú and Maureen were left alone in the cottage. There were only a few hours until dawn and they had no idea what the day would bring.

Maureen did not know what to say. Conversation usually came quite easily, but now it seemed awkward. She began to busy herself putting together another place to sleep for the night, as Maitiú needed the cot to rest. She added to the turf fire to keep them warm until dawn. She then brought him another basin of cold water and mixed the herbs that Sara had left to help ease the swelling on his face. As she rinsed a cloth in cold water, he reached over and took her hand.

"'Tis alright Maureen, truly. 'Tis not yer fault. Now stop stumblin' around and get some rest." She was exhausted and heartbroken. She sat down on the floor in front of him.

"But it be all me fault. Look at ya Maitiú, look what they done to ya. I be so sorry me friend. I swear I had no idea that..." He stopped her at that.

"Let it go for tonight lass. Tomorrow we shall seek counsel with Heber as Cullen planned and we be getting' this set to right. Now get some rest. Besides Maureen, a sto'r, ya can nay hurt an Irishman by hittin' him on the head." He gave a chuckle and a smile, followed by a grimace. He slowly and painfully laid back down on the cot, placing the towel back on his battered face.

But rest would not come this night. Danger lurked in the shire, Maureen's friends were in peril and she was the cause of it. No, rest would not come this night.

The dawn broke on the Sabbath morn to a bright and beautiful day. No matter the troubles of men and women, the Earth Mother pays no mind and the world goes on in all its wonder. Maureen had barely slept at all. She should have taken some of the valerian tea Sara had left for Maitiú to help him rest. With all the swelling to Maitiú's face, he snored up a storm. Between that and the simple fact that she was frightened who may be lurking nearby made it impossible to rest. She grabbed her stable apron and headed off to morning chores. Since Maitiú had taken the ponies with him for the ale cart sometime back, there were only a few horses at the stable besides Olaf, and cleaning and caring for them would not take too long. She missed the ponies, as did Olaf. But for now, only Olaf, Chieftain's and Morna's horses were regulars.

Sir Teague and Lady Seaton's horses were also stabled, as they had remained in the Shire following the Queen's departure.

They had been meeting with Heber and met with the Queen together during Her Majesty's progress to the shire. Katie had tried to needle Phillip for information about their meeting, but that did not work, for he honestly did not know what was going on. Even Elena could not find out, and if she could not get Heber to talk, no one could.

With only five stalls to clean, feed and water, Maureen would be done in no time. Then back to the cottage to collect Maitiú and off to the tavern. Her only regret was that she would be unable to celebrate Mass this day. She and Maitiú both agreed that it would not be safe, for Armstrong's men would most certainly be watching the church.

She saw no one on her way to the stables, but it was early and even scoundrels need to sleep. She opened the door to the tack room and placed her basket of carrots on the table. She walked over to greet Olaf, but something was wrong. He was uneasy and would not let her pass his stall to get to the other horses. He bowed his head down towards her and gently pushed her back away from other horses. She knew her horse well and he was trying to warn her. Someone was hiding in the stalls at the end of the stable. She kissed him on the nose and thanked him, gathered her basket from the tack room and hurried back to the cottage.

She ran as fast as she could back to the cottage. When she burst through the door, Maitiú flew off the cot and landed square on his arse on the floor. After letting out a very loud groan from the pain, he raised himself back up on the cot.

"Damn girl, can ya come through the door like a normal person?"

"Someone was in the stable Maitiú! I ran back as fast as I could. I may have been followed, I do nay know for sure, I did nay see and..."

"Slow down lass," he said. "Slow down now. Calm yerself girl and tell me what happened." She relayed the events to Maitiú.

"You saw no one behind ya?" he asked.

"Nay, I did not. But I did nay look, I just ran."

"We need to get to the tavern," he said. "Let's hurry now."

"But Maitiú, ya can nay just walk out of here. If they see ya, they be knowin' ya escaped alive." He looked at her with a puzzled look on his face.

"Do nay worry," she said. "I know just what to do."

She went to her trunk and brought out an extra shirt, shawl and bodice. When she turned to Maitiú with the clothes he said, "Hold on now girl, I'll not be donin' a bloody skirt."

After a bit of argument, he finally agreed to put the skirt over his trews and wrap the shawl over his head. He would however, have nothing to do with the bodice. After he was dressed, with the shawl over his head, he turned to Maureen as they were heading out the door. She tried her hardest, but even with the situation as dire as it was, she just could not help it. She broke into full out laughter. He did not find it funny at all.

They left the cottage and started across the field to the tavern. Maitiú had not been up and around much, and going was slow as he was still in much pain from the night before. It looked as if Maureen was helping a crippled old woman to the tavern for Sara to tend with medicinals.

When they entered the tavern, everyone turned to look. When Maitiú removed the shawl from his head a few snickers began, until they saw his face. No one was laughing after that. Elena helped Maitiú to a comfortable chair and brought him some hot tea and a shot of whiskey.

Lord Cullen had already arrived and was in counsel with Chieftain Heber. Philip had returned along with Katie. Elena was present, but the Tánaiste was not yet in the tavern. Lady Gwendolyn had gone to the Chapel to check on Maire and speak with Father Desmond.

Philip had immediately put two-and-two together. When he saw his Irish friend, he knew that the blood he had seen on MacLeod's hands the night before belonged to the bogtrotter, and that MacLeod was the one who had given him this beating. The warrior-poet was filled with rage and vengeance for his longtime companion.

Maureen immediately went to the safety of Katie's arms. Katie was her kin and her friend, and she longed for Katie's calming warmth and comfort.

Philip looked toward Maitiú with profound sorrow for the looks of his friend, and rage for the bastards who did it.

"Maitiú a chara, this will nay go unanswered," vowed Philip.

"I be glad for your words, but I be not wantin' ya to get in trouble on my account. But ya might want to get in trouble on Her Majesty's account," Maitiú replied.

Everyone looked puzzled and Philip said, "Stop with the riddles and speak plainly man!"

Maitiú continued, "The cute amadans are plotting against Mary Stuart. They be fookin' agents for that Saxon whore."

Everyone in the room who knew Maitiú, knew he was referring to Her Royal Majesty Queen Elizabeth I of England. Near exasperation Philip pleaded, "What did they say man?"

"Well, I was layin' face down in the mud when I came to. I was covered in blood, so they must have thought I was dead. I heard them say that me Maire got away and so I decided I was in no hurry to get up. So, I just lay there ya know, still as a stone."

Cullen interrupted, "Have ya ever known an Irishman to make a long story short?"

Heber added, "Nay, but I've known them to make a short story long."

As everyone chuckled, Maitiú continued, "As I was sayin', while I was lying in the mud, they started talkin' ya know. How they needed to finish this chore up, get back to England and report to the Queen's advisor, some blaggard by the name of Cecil, William Cecil. MacLeod was jawin' about gettin' his hands on his gold, how they would be well off when they got back to England and in good favor with the Queen."

"Ya be certain of this man? Yer brain's not been addled by the beatin' ya took has it?" Heber questioned Maitiú sternly.

"Aye, MacPherson, I be sure indeed. What be their errand for the Saxon Queen, I can nay say."

With that, Heber immediately sent a messenger for Sir Teague and Lady Seaton. They must get word to the Queen's Halberdiers. These men were traitors to the Crown of Scotland and presented a very real danger to Mary Stuart. They must be stopped.

"There be more." The Irishman's voice lowered a bit. "They be hell bent on findin' this gold. They be of a mind Maureen's the one hidin' it, and they have little intention of leavin' her around to tell anyone about it."

Heber and Cullen exchanged glances, and both turned their gaze toward Maureen.

She buried her face in Katie's shoulder. How could this have happened? How could things have gone so wrong?

The door to the Wycked Aye opened and the Tánaiste entered. She walked immediately over to the Chieftain. He leaned back and turned an ear toward her. She whispered something to him and he nodded his head in acknowledgment.

As she came back around the table toward Maureen, she tapped her on the knee and said, "Come with me lass, we still have a tavern to run. Yer chores will take yer mind off yer troubles."

Maureen looked at Katie and she gave her a nudge

and said, "Off ya go now, I be right behind ya."

"But...," Maureen hesitated. "I have yet to finish tendin' the horses Mistress. Someone was hidin' in the stables when I went for mornin' chores. I ran back for Maitiú and we came straight here. They still need to be cared for."

"I be tendin' the horses for ya lass, do nay worry over it," Philip snapped. He was pacing the room, still wild with anger for the violence inflicted upon his friend. Maureen nodded in agreement and followed Mistress Morna to the pantry to begin the day's preparations for the tavern. Katie was not far behind. It was clear it was time to leave the men alone with the Chieftain to make their plans.

Lord and Lady Seaton were seated at a small table at the back of the common room at the Inn. Lady Seaton sat quietly as she picked over a breakfast of ham, biscuits and boiled eggs. Her mind was baffled with the events of late. She had been confronted with Robert MacLeod many times on campaign. She had suspected he was a traitor to Scotland and the Isles but had no proof. But she had other reasons to despise him, reasons that fueled a personal vengeance she would see satisfied. And now he was within her reach. But why was he here she pondered, certainly not to reunite with his daughter. One thing she was sure of, was that MacLeod had no love for family or any concern for the women he used and abandoned. Women he would force himself on and then leave them alone and with child. He was a predator of a disgusting nature. But why was he here now, during the Queen's progress? Why had he not moved on? Why was he still lingering around?

"Cailín...Cailín! Where's yer mind wife?" Her husband's voice brought her back to the moment. Although they had only been married a short time, they knew each other well and had never held any secrets from one another. Cailín had no intention of hiding her concerns about MacLeod from her husband. Robert MacLeod was a demon from her past for certain, but he may also be a danger to the Queen, and that was Sir Teague's arena.

"Forgive me, Teague. I must tell ya me husband, on me errand for Her Majesty, I spied a man in the crowd who..."

"Sir Teague!" Young Grady from the tavern interrupted. "Forgive me interruption M' Lord, but Chieftain Heber requests yer presence at the tavern. 'Tis a matter of urgency."

"Pray, what be wrong lad?" questioned Sir Teague.

Grady lowered his voice, "Her Majesty may be in danger." Teague and Cailín immediately rose from their table, gathered their swords and followed Grady back to the Wycked Aye.

The traitors had moved the ale wagon to the outskirts of the shire during the wee hours of the morning. The ponies had been unhitched and were tied to trees by the pond nearby. As they rested near the cart, the errand boy they had sent to stables returned.

"I see ya return empty handed boy. Where be the girl?" asked Armstrong

"I waited like ya said. She showed up early to tend to the stables, but somethin' tipped her off. That stallion of hers seemed spooked, she got nervous and left," reported the minion. "I never had a chance to get a hold of her."

Armstrong grumbled, "Ah, that damn black, devil horse of hers. I swear it bloody talks to her. I do nay know which one of them I would prefer to be dead, that devil horse or yer dagger carryin' bitch of a girl-child."

MacLeod chuckled, "Me daughter too much fer ya to handle man?"

"Nay not, but she be a bothersome little wretch fer certain and she be wastin' our time. We need to finish this MacLeod and get back to England. This had damn well better be worth the risk," warned Armstrong.

"Oh, I can assure ya," MacLeod replied. "It be worth it."

By the time Lord & Lady Seaton arrived back at the Wycked Aye, most of the Highlanders had already gathered. Lady Morna's early morning call to arms had been well received. Connor, Braden, Master Thomas and Lady Isabella, Oliver and Fiona were present to name just a few. When Braden arrived, Cullen went to greet his brother, grateful for his help for Braden was one of the finest swordsmen in the Highlands. As all were settling in, Lady Gwen returned from Chapel and went immediately to Maitiú.

"Maire be safe and well, cousin, but concerned for her Da. Father Desmond suggests that she stay safely in the convent until this matter be finished."

Maitiú nodded in agreement, "Aye, 'twould be for the best for sure. Besides, I do nay want her to see her Da lookin' like this."

Lady Gwen gave him a look over and said, "Are ya referrin' to yer face or yer skirts cousin?"

Maitiú looked down and realized he was still wearing Maureen's skirt.

"That be not a bit funny, Gwendolyn," he replied.

"Oh, aye it most certainly is," she countered.

Chieftain had taken Sir Teague aside and shared the information Maitiú had given him earlier. As Captain of the Queen's Guard, Sir Teague would be the one to decide the next course of action.

"It be clear Chieftain that we must take care of this business before we proceed on our own errand for Her Majesty. These men must nay be allowed to return to England." Teague was thinking out loud. "The Queen's safety is of greatest importance. Pray, where be the servant girl now?"

"She be in the back workin' with the Tánaiste," Heber replied. He did not care for the implication in Sir Teague's voice. It was clear that there would be little concern for the safety of young Mistress MacLeod. Heber knew full well that the Queen's welfare came first. But he liked his little green-eyed wildcat and did not want to see her put in danger. Besides, she was one of the best workers he ever had in the tavern.

"Good, she can just be stayin' there for now," replied Sir Teague. "I will send me new Halberdier, Oliver Ross, on to Holyrood Castle to inform Captain Somerville of this situation. We must move quickly to apprehend these men and get on with our own mission for Her Majesty. Now MacPherson, let us speak with the Highlanders and make our plans."

Heber nodded in agreement and they went off to speak with the others.

Meg, Morna, Katie and Maureen were in the pantry preparing for the day's patrons, as well as serving the Highlanders who had responded to Heber's call. These people were loyal to the Chieftain and were loyal subjects to Her Majesty, Mary Stuart.

Morna had been right, the work was good and did take Maureen's mind off of all this mess for a while. But her heart was heavy, for now she knew that not only was her father a greedy, heartless murder, he was a warloghe, a traitor to the Crown of Scotland. It was almost too much to bear.

Master Thomas Campbell had approached Maitiú upon arrival. After conveying his sympathies, he said, "You know, Irishman, on our way to the tavern, I spotted two Connemara ponies tied up just outside of town near the old pond. They would nay happen ta be yers now would they?"

Maitiú looked at him with great interest.

"Maybe you and I should take a gander out that way and bring em' home, what say ya?" asked Thomas.

"Aye," responded Maitiú. "I be willing to bet that me ale cart would be lingerin' somewhere nearby as well."

"Count me in on that one," chimed Philip. "I not be lettin' ya out of me sight, Bogmouse."

Everyone had gathered in the main hall of the tavern.

"Good marrow good gentles and thanks be to ya all for coming to arms," Heber began. He shared the situation with all who had gathered and then the discussions began on how to capture these men and bring them to justice. Back and forth the conversations went until finally a woman's voice rang through.

"Release the lamb," it was Lady Seaton.

"Beg Pardon, M' Lady?" questioned Heber.

"Release the lamb," she replied. Everyone stopped talking and turned to listen. Lady Seaton rose from her place at the table to speak.

"'Twould appear these traitors have completed their chore for the Saxon Queen. What holds them here now be of a personal nature. So, we give them what they be lookin' for. Release the lamb, 'twill nay take long for the wolves to find her."

"So, ya want ta be sendin' Mistress MacLeod out as bait then?" asked Connor. "I do nay like it, I do nay like it at all," he said.

Until now, none of the other women had spoken.

"Neither do I," exclaimed Morna. "Heber, this can nay be born! 'Tis far too dangerous for the lass, there must be another way."

Maureen moved closer to Katie and Katie put her arms around Maureen's shoulders. They both looked to Philip and Maitiú. Maitiú dropped his glance and Maureen knew he was praying. Philip looked at Katie with an expression that told her clearly he had no choice in the matter. Heber did not have time to respond to the Tánaiste. Sir Teague moved to the center of the discussion.

"There be plenty of men here to keep an eye on the lass, and we can nay allow these traitors to return to England. Whatever information they have can nay be allowed to make its way to Queen Elizabeth or her advisors." Everyone nodded in agreement with Sir Teague.

Maureen felt Katie pull her closer as Heber rose from his table and began to come toward them.

"No," cried Katie. "No, you can nay do this, please Heber." Maureen turned to Katie and gently pulled away from her embrace.

"'Tis alright cousin. I'll do it. It must be done," she whispered to Katie. She turned to face her Chieftain.

Heber placed his hands on her shoulders, "These be good men, Maureen. They be watchin' out for ya. Keep yer dagger with ya lass. Pull it from the sheath and put it in yer boot. The cover on that blade be far too tight and ya would not be able to draw it in time if ya needed it," Heber warned in a caring and fatherly manner.

He was right. Master Brady had fashioned a fine new sheath for her doe-hoofed dagger, but the sheath was tight and you could not pull the dagger quickly. She took the dagger from her belt, and slipped the bare blade into her boot.

"Now, go on about yer chores girl, the lads here will be around wherever ya go," Heber said softly. She looked up to meet the big man's eyes. He embraced her and said, "Ya mind yerself now girl, keep yer wits about ya."

"I will Heber, do nay worry over it," Maureen replied.

The Chieftain hesitated as if he had much more to say, but then he turned and walked back to his table. He had a final word with his men and then the Highland warriors left the tavern to take their positions about the shire.

Maureen walked over to Philip, "Do nay be botherin' with the horses, Philip. 'Tis me job and I be seein' to it as soon as I finish up here. Nothin' like shovelin' horse apples to take yer mind off yer troubles." She forced a smile and went on about her duties.

Lady Seaton pulled her husband aside, "We must speak my love, before this goes any farther. There be much I need ta tell ya."

Her husband looked at her with concern, then placed his arm around her waist and led her to a private place to talk. It was time for Cailín Seaton to share a chapter of her past that she did not enjoy recalling and her reasons for an intense hatred towards a man she had been hunting for a very long time.

Philip, Thomas and Maitiú had piled into Master Thomas' cart and were headed towards the outskirts of the shire to recover the ale cart, the ponies and, hopefully, the ale. None of the men were carrying any obvious weapons. Philip did have his dirk and Thomas had an axe in the bottom of the cart. Master Thomas was the butcher in the shire and was far more skilled with an axe in his hands than a broadsword. But their plan was not one of battle. It was one of stealth and cunning, a simple matter of stealing back what was rightfully theirs.

As they reached the outskirts of the shire, Thomas directed their attention toward the old pond. Aye and for certain, there were Maitiú's ponies tied to the trees.

"There they be Irish, those be yer ponies?" asked Thomas.

"Saints be praised, they most certainly be me little fillies. Let's hide the cart over near that hedge of rowan and have a look about," said Maitiú. They pulled the cart behind a tall hedge of rowan and tied off the reins.

"Lads, here ya go," Master Thomas handed a flask to Philip.

"If we get killed, at least we be havin' a wee dram of fine whiskey before we go." Philip chuckled and took a tip of the flask then handed it over to Maitiú, who did the same.

The men crept through the forest, making their way toward the ponies and the old pond. Maitiú was being as quiet as a mouse, but the other two were like listening to a full regiment marching through the forest.

"Quiet now, you two sound like cattle trompin' through the forest," whispered Maitiú.

"We nay be a bogtrotter like you, ya know," returned Philip.

When they arrived near the ponies, Maitiú signaled the other two to stay put while he approached the horses.

"Good marrow me lovelies," Maitiú whispered to the horses in Gaelic. The ponies did not startle, but rustled their heads from side-to-side as if they were glad to see their keeper once again.

Maitiú motioned the other men forward where they knelt down and hid behind the horses. As they peered into the traitors' encampment, they could see the ale cart was next to a small cluster of chestnut trees. There was no sign of Armstrong or MacLeod, but Armstrong's two ruffians and a servant boy were still in camp.

"Ah, one fer each of us," whispered Thomas.

"That one over there by the cart," Maitiú whispered. "That one be mine."

"As you wish. And you Philip, any preference fer ya?" questioned Thomas.

"I be takin' the servant boy by the campfire," Philip replied.

"Well met, then the poor sap asleep by the tree be all mine," chuckled Thomas.

When Maitiú had seen the man by the cart, he recognized him as one of the amadans who had a hold of his daughter while MacLeod and Armstrong were beating on him. Maitiú's Irish blood was at full boil. He waited patiently until he saw Philip's quarry pulled from the campfire and into the bushes. Then, Master Thomas snatched the blaggard sleeping by the tree and he too disappeared into the thick hedge of rowan. Now it was Maitiú's turn.

His man was bent over, fiddling with the rigging on the cart. Maitiú quietly sneaked up behind him and tapped him on the shoulder. When he turned and saw Maitiú's face he looked like he had seen a bloody ghost. Maitiú doubled up his right fist and clocked the blaggard square in the jaw. The bloke never knew what hit him. His knees gave a bit of a wobble and he fell to the ground like a rock.

Maitiú stood over him and said, "Ha! How do ya like that one boyo! Not bad for a dead man aye?" The man opened his eyes and looked up.

Maitiú leaned a little closer and said, "That be what ya get fer puttin' yer dirty, thievin' hands on me daughter. I see ya anywhere near her again and I be runnin' ya through meself." The man's eyes rolled back and he passed out cold.

Philip walked up beside his friend, "I imagine that felt pretty damn good."

"It did indeed," replied Maitiú.

Thomas came up as well, "I see ya put that one flat on his arse." Thomas gave Maitiú a slap on the back, which caused him to grimace a bit.

"Come on, we'll hitch up the cart and be ready to roll. Oh, and good news Irish, they never even cracked the ale kegs."

"Off we go lads. Let's get this cart back to the Wycked Aye before the traitors return," warned Philip. "And I do believe it would be quite fittin' to deliver these blaggards to Sir Teague."

Thomas drove his cart containing the three sleeping amadans who were now bruised, bound and gagged. Phillip and Maitiú drove the ale cart with two fine, new horses in tow. The lads were of a mind that their previous owners would not be having much of a need for horses where they would be going. With any luck, they would be back to the tavern by dusk and be having a pint from one of the kegs by nightfall.

Maureen had only an hour or so of chores left at the tavern. As she cleaned up tables, Mistress Meg came up to her.

"He had no choice. Ya know that lass," she said.

"Aye, I understand full well," Maureen replied. "I be finishin' up here shortly Mistress Meg and be headin' off to the stable. The horses must be starvin' by now."

"Be careful lass and check with the Tánaiste before ya go," she replied.

Maureen took her tray of tankards back to the

pantry for washing. She began to put the mugs in for washing and rinsing. Katie and Sara were both at her side before she could finish the first batch.

"So, will ya be goin' over to the stables after this?" asked Sara. "We can go with ya, we can help with the horses and..."

"Sara, 'tis most kind of ya indeed, but I will nay be seein' ya put in danger," Maureen said. "Besides, we need ya here in case...well, we need ya here."

"Please cousin, do nay go alone. Let one of the men go with ya," pleaded Katie.

"No, Lady Seaton be right," she said. "'Tis me they be after. If the men be too close by, they will nay take the bait."

They finished washing and drying the tankards. Maureen checked with Morna and she had nothing more for her to do. It was time for her to go.

"I do nay like it, I do nay like it all," Morna was mumbling as she moved through the pantry. "Ya mind yerself girl. Ya hear me!"

"Aye Tánaiste, I hear ya loud and clear," Maureen replied.

The Highlander men had left the tavern and were out and about the shire waiting and watching. Lady Seaton had left the tavern as well to take care of some errands after finishing her long talk with Sir Teague.

Maureen grabbed some carrots from the pantry and put them in her basket. She gathered her things and headed over to the stables.

She saw no one along the way to stables; everything seemed so normal. But she knew that around the corners and in the shadows waited the brave men of the Highlands.

It was mid-afternoon when she reached the

stables. She entered the tack room and was placing her basket of carrots on the floor next to the table, when she heard the door creak and then close behind her. Hiding behind the door was Ian Armstrong.

"'bout bloody arse time ya got here," he snarled. She bolted for the door and he shoved her back against the table.

"Yer not goin' anywhere, missy. You and I, we have a dance to finish and yer goin' to pay up this time. Then, yer goin' to give me that chest of gold of yer Da's and I'll be on me way with everything that be owed to me."

He came up behind her and wrapped his arms around her chest. He began to run his hands over her bodice and pull at her skirts. The hatred and rage grew inside her like a firestorm. She had been forced to suffer through this disgrace once before and swore she would never suffer through it again. It had earned Armstrong the scar across his face and nearly cost her her life from the beating he gave her afterwards. If it cost her life this time, she cared not. She would not allow it to happen again.

Armstrong had her pressed face down on the table, her left arm pinned behind her back. She could feel his disgusting and vial breath on her neck. With her free hand she slowly and carefully reached down to pull her doe-hoofed dagger from her boot.

"God forgive me," she said to herself. She rolled over on her back and wrapped her legs around his hips.

"Well, that be more like it ya little whore," he said.

"Aye, it is indeed ya filthy toad," she replied. And with that, she plunged her dagger into his belly as far as it would go. He yelled out in pain and tried to pull away, but her legs had him locked in, he could not escape. She quickly put her other hand to the hilt of the dagger and forced it upward straight into his black heart. That finished it. Blood gushed from his chest covering her arms and clothes. He was choking and spitting up blood. She released her legs, put a boot to his chest, pushing him off her and off the blade. He fell to the floor dead.

She laid back on the table and let out a weak and painful moan. She was shaking and felt very cold. She raised herself from the table and tried to stand but her legs were weak and unsteady. Her clothes were soaked in Armstrong's blood. She looked at the dagger in her hand and began to tremble uncontrollably. She fell to her knees, "Dear God, what have I done?"

She felt sick as she struggled to raise herself from the floor to go for help. But when she turned to head for the door blocking the doorway stood her father. It was the first time she had seen him in many years, and at that moment, she had no desire to see him at all.

"Let me go Father!" she screamed as she tried to push her way past him.

He grabbed her by her shoulders, lifting her off the ground and shook her.

"Now be that any way to greet yer Da after all these years?" he snidely replied. "Yer not goin' anywhere daughter. Now where be it? Where be the chest ya took?" he growled.

"I do nay know what yer talkin' about. I do nay have it." It was a lie for certain, but she would not betray the only man who had ever shown her kindness. She would not give up her Chieftain to this traitor.

He backhanded her across the face and shook her again. Her nose began to bleed and her mouth was cut as well.

"Do nay lie to me ya little bitch, where be the gold?" He pulled her up to his face and yelled, "Where be it!?"

She could not speak. She was frozen with fear. All she could think of was that she was going to die at the hands of her father. Then suddenly, his body jolted, he gasped and a blank look crossed his face. His grip weakened, releasing her, and she tumbled to the ground.

As she turned back to look, she could see the tip of a Rapier piercing through his chest as his shirt ran with blood. As his legs gave way, his head fell forward and his body slid off of the sword, crumbling on the ground before her.

Behind him, with sword in hand, stood Lady Cailín Seaton. Her face showed no emotion, she did not speak. She simply pulled a cloth from her belt and began to clean her sword. As she wiped the blood from the blade, she looked toward the body of the man before her and said, "You shall never disgrace another Irish woman."

It was only a short time before the commotion drew the attention of the men nearby. They ran through the stables, causing all of the horses to spook and bolt in their stalls. Heber was calling out to Maureen but she could not answer. They burst through the tack room door to find her collapsed on the floor next to Armstrong, and Lady Seaton standing over the body of Robert MacLeod.

Sir Teague approached and stood behind her. "What goes on here wife?" he asked.

"Justice, my husband, justice," she replied. "These

traitors are no longer a threat to our Queen," then she turned her gaze to Maureen, "Or to anyone."

Maureen could not speak, she simply bowed her head to Lady Seaton in thanks. Lady Seaton raised her sword to her forehead in a gesture of honor, then turned and walked to the side of her husband. She sheathed her sword and as she turned to face him, a single tear ran down her cheek. He gently wiped the tear from her face. He understood, no more need be said.

He turned to Heber, "MacPherson, I will leave this mess for ya to tend. Do with them what ya will." He put his arm around his lady and led her away.

"Take them to the gallows and string them up," Heber proclaimed. "Let it be known to all what we do to traitors here in the Highlands."

Heber went to Maureen where she lay on the tack room floor.

"Are ya hurt lass?" he asked gently.

She looked up at him with tears in her eyes. Her nose and mouth were still bleeding.

"I be alright, Chieftain. Everything be alright now."

He gently scooped her up from the floor and carried her to back to the tavern.

To the others, Lady Seaton had dispatched a traitor to the Crown of Scotland. For Maureen, she and Lady Seaton had slain two demons that had long haunted both of their lives.

Chapter Six

MacPherson's Away

www.thesonofscotland.co.uk

The young lad came bursting into the Wycked Aye and rushed past the barman and the ladies working that day before they could say a word. He went straight to the Chieftain's table and, in a flourish of words, began to babble, "My Lord, I have been sent by the priest at the chapel. Maitiú de Faoite, the brewer, has been abducted by Portuguese sailors. They are pressing him upon their ship. Déan deifer, hurry!"

Heber quickly adjusted his attention and took in all that was transpiring. The lad was a rangy sort, his clothes a bit tattered. His size and bearing were that of a ten or twelve-year-old boy, but his eyes looked much older. If his story was true, Heber would have to make haste; and if not, a brisk jaunt down to the quay would do him no harm. He grabbed his sword and scabbard, and without a word went straight out the door.

The lad waited a moment until MacPherson turned the corner and slunk back into the shadows where he came. There, waiting as promised, was the dark-haired foreign sailor with the gold coin that would feed his mother, brothers and sisters for a month.

Portuguese ship was moored on the quay. It had one guard who, upon seeing the MacPherson approach, stepped lightly aside. Heber assumed the guard fled in terror and so his entire attention was on bounding up the gangway to rescue his friend. He didn't see the club hidden under the guard's cloak. With great force, it came down upon his head. Heber felt the stinging blow and saw the flash of red and blue lights and then oblivion...darkness.

When he awoke it was dark and damp. It reeked of dead fish, vomit and urine. When his eyes finally focused, he surmised he was in the bottom of a ship. The chains on his arms and legs confirmed his initial thought; he was the one who was pressed.

Two weeks passed and Heber was able to discern from his fellow shipmates that they were bound for Lisbon. Other than the chains, he was well fed and allowed on the deck for exercise when the seas were calm. Maitiú was not on board and it soon became clear what his fate would be.

King Sebastian of Portugal was trying to gain favor with the Pope and prove what a fine Christian gentleman he was. He was gathering an army of like-minded gentlemen to wage war on the heretical Moors. Perhaps the Holy Father didn't know, or didn't want to know, how many of these Christian gentlemen came to be recruited.

At that moment, with chains off and sword in hand, Heber knew escape was not an option. It would be prudent to bide his time and make the best of a bad situation. The sailors who brought Heber aboard were well compensated for bringing such a fierce fighting man into their company.

The Scots and especially the Irish were desired members of any European army. They withstood privation without complaint, accepted less pay and fought with amazing ferocity and tenacity.

Heber was surveying his fellow comrades when he saw a stocky Irish lad in a saffron léine who looked vaguely familiar. These Irish lads had been trained in Rome by Italian gunners and thought they were bound to Ireland to liberate old Erin from Saxon tyranny. Instead they too were pressed into Sebastian's service. When the lad's eyes met Heber's there was a light shown up in them. Then, in the accent of Munster Gaelic, Heber heard the lad say, "An bhfeiceann tú sin anois? Tú féin atá ann! It be me Da's old friend, Heber MacPherson, come to save us all!"

Heber knew then and there, that all thoughts of his escape were to be abandoned. He would remain in this enterprise, if for no other reason than to shield young Dónal MacMaitiú de Faoite, his best friend's son, from the savage Moors and the desert sands of that hell called Morocco.

Chapter Seven

Turn of the Wheel

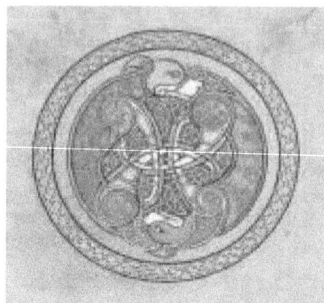

www.ancienttrails.com

It had been almost ten days since Heber had disappeared. Stolen they said, bundled off on a ship to God knows where.

Fionnula had been devastated by her husband's disappearance. She was lost without the big man by her side. She did her best to continue with her obligations to the tavern, but it was just no use. She needed to be with her family, whether it be for support in the hope of Heber's return or in morning for his loss. That was where she wanted to be. And so, she had made arrangements to return to Ireland on the next ship leaving from Dumbarton.

Maureen had spent most of her free time at chapel trying to make sense of it all. So much had happened. All she could do was to pray that God had taken Heber for some greater purpose. That he would return safe and well.

The tavern was not as it was when she had first come to the Wycked Aye. Katie had gone back to Skye as her cousin Andrew's health was failing, and she missed her more than anyone could ever know. Mistress Morna was leaving too, going off to Dornoch to be with her sister Brittah Sutherland H'elie, and on to Court with the Queen.

Dame Brittah Sutherland H'elie, who owned the Wycked Aye Tavern, had entrusted its proprietorship to Heber for many years. He ran a fine tavern and made a goodly profit for Lady Sutherland. Now, with Heber gone missing, Her Ladyship still had a business to run and would be appointing a new proprietor, a new tavern Chieftain to manage and care for it. But for now, all who had come to love and respect Chieftain Heber MacPherson were still holding on to the hope he would return.

Maureen felt a tap on her shoulder as she was finishing her prayers.

"Ya been here a long time lass. You're goin' ta wear the beads right off of that Rosary, girl." Father Brian Desmond sat down next to her. "God will watch over Heber, do nay worry."

"I pray he will Father, but I have a bad feelin' in me heart. It just seems so much sadness has touched our shire and there have been so many changes in the tavern. I feel lost Father."

Father Desmond offered her a hand to help raise her off her knees. She sat down beside him on the bench on the commoner's side of the chapel. He took both her hands and held them between his. His hands were strong and comforting. Father Brian was near the same age as Maitiú. Red haired and green-eyed, he was a fit and able man, and quite handsome.

"Ya have been through great trials in yer young life child," he said. "But those are over now. 'Tis time to end yer grievin' and move on with yer life. Yer penance is done. Now go on over to the tavern and have some fun with yer friends."

She raised her eyes to meet his and saw the kindness and warmth that she had always seen in the eyes of her parish priest. She gave him a smile and said, "thank ya Father and peace be with ya."

"And with you," he returned. "And I do nay want to be seein' ya until the Sabbath, and be sure ta bring that Irishman with ya when ya come."

She had only gone a short distance when she remembered Mistress Morna had asked her to pick up a few things from Master Maguire's apothecary. She had lost track of time in the Chapel and was now running late, as usual. She spun around and headed back down the lane as fast as she could.

Maureen arrived at Master Liam's shop and flew through the door like a whirlwind.

"Do nay tell me, let me guess. Runnin' late again are ya?" Master Liam said with a bit of a chuckle in his voice.

"Aye Master Liam that I am, I have a list from Mistress Morna. She be havin' me head on a spit if I do nay come back with her medicinals."

She gave him the list. He took a look over it and then went about putting together the various items Morna had requested.

"Tell Mistress MacGregor I be havin' to send over one or two of these items, do nay have them in at present. I be sorry to see her go ya know. Lucky our little shire has been to have two grand healers all to ourselves. She and Sara McBride have cared for damn near everyone in this shire at one time or another. But she can nay turn down a request from the Queen, can she now?"

He was right. Sara and Morna had been the healers and surgeons for the Shire for as long as most people could remember. They had birthed babies, cured fevers and sewn up wounded Highlanders after battle. Maureen doubted there was a court surgeon who could hold a candle to either one of them. She herself had learned a great deal from helping them with the shire folk that came to them with their various afflictions. Dame Brittah had made mention of this fact to the Queen and now Her Majesty had sent a messenger carrying an appointment to Court, requesting Morna's presence and services as the Royal Apothecary while Her Majesty traveled on progress. And no one turns down a request from the Queen.

Finally, Master Liam came to the counter with the assorted pouches, bottles and packets of herbs, barks and oils; some for the tavern, some not.

"So, were ya out ridin' again Maureen, that why ya be runnin' late?" he asked. She hesitated and answered quietly, "Nay, Master Liam, I was at chapel."

"Ah," he too paused for a moment. "So, there be no word then?"

"No word sir, no news at all," she replied. He nodded his head in understanding. She thanked him for his help, paid for Morna's wares, and headed to the tavern.

When Maureen arrived, she found Mistress Morna sitting alone at the Chieftain's great table. A large parcel sat before her and she had a missive in her hands.

"Mistress Morna, are ya alright? Ya look as if yer mind be wonderin'. I have most of the medicinals ya asked for. Master Lian will bring the rest later." She did not respond, simply nodded her head in acknowledgment. It was clear this was no time for talking and that Morna was upset by the missive she had received. Maureen placed the potions on the table and went to check with Mistress Sara for her duties for the evening.

Sara was in the pantry going over the stock on the shelves. When Maureen asked her about Morna, Sara explained that a messenger had delivered both the parcel and the missive from her sister. Dame Brittah would be arriving in three days with her entourage to collect Morna and take her back to Dornoch in County Sutherland. Dame Brittah would also be securing a new proprietor for the tavern during the Chieftain's absence and a new Tánaiste as well.

"Well, it all sounds so well and good now does is not Sara?" Maureen said sarcastically. "I can tell ya one thing for damn sure, it bloody does nay feel well or good to me," Maureen grumbled under her breath.

"There be not much we can do about change, lass. Everything changes, none of us can stop that." Sara's words were true for sure. She was a strong and wise woman. "Now, would ya like to get out there and get to it. We still have a tavern to run, ya know," she said with bit of a smile.

"Aye, Sara, I be gettin' to it. Yer startin' to sound like Morna."

Everyone was dressed in their best when Dame Brittah Sutherland H'elie arrived. Her entourage of servants, footmen and attendants was impressive to say the least. Morna had assembled all of the tavern workers for her inspection, and Master Thomas had seen to it that a fine lamb was on the spit and the cook pots were full when she arrived.

It was clear that Dame Brittah was not a woman to be trifled with. She was a sight to behold in her fine noble gown, but it was clear from her demeanor that she was a business woman. She had enough energy for herself and ten more. She was deliberate and direct, and had the attention of everyone in the tavern from the moment she entered.

To everyone's surprise, others had been summoned by Dame Brittah to the tavern, as well, and began to arrive soon after: Lord Cullen Elliot, Sir Teague Seaton and Sir Duncan Somerville, to name a few. After inspecting the tavern and its staff, Dame Brittah met with the noblemen and guardsmen who had arrived, a meeting behind closed doors.

When they emerged, the noblemen paid their proper respects to Dame Brittah and left the tavern. Apparently, their meeting had been productive and that an alliance had been drawn. The tavern staff was informed that she and her sister would be retiring for the afternoon and that they would be departing in two days' time. Morna would be leaving in two days.

Maureen sighed and her shoulders slumped when she heard that Morna would be leaving soon. Fionnula had only been gone for a short time and now Morna would be gone in two days. She could feel her tavern family slipping away from her. What would happen when a new Chieftain was named? Would she still be given shelter as Heber had given her or would she be dismissed? She was filled with fear and uncertainty as she watched Dame Brittah and Morna retire to their chamber.

Those two days passed by faster than many would have liked. Dame Brittah had placed Sara McBride in charge of the tavern. Sara had requested that Lady Isabella Campbell be named as her Tánaiste and so it was agreed. Sara would make a fine Chieftain, she was a fair and stern woman. She held the loyalty of the Highland men who were allied to Heber, and knew she could depend on them to help keep the peace in the tavern. Heber MacPherson had always taken pride in the fact that the Wycked Aye was a place of peace and joy, and neutrality. All folk were welcome no matter their faith, clan or political alliance and Chieftain Sara intended to keep it that way.

None of the girls had been given a chance to speak with Morna since Lady Sutherland had arrived. They all had wishes and sentiments they longed to express to a fine woman with whom they had spent many a long night. A woman they had all come to love. But that was not to be had. Finally, the time came for Dame Brittah and Morna to leave. All were assembled to say goodbye. Gasps went through the line as they all laid eyes upon their former Tánaiste.

"Damn, will ya look at that, she looks beautiful," Fiona whispered to Maureen as they stood in line waiting to give her well wishes.

Beautiful she was, dressed in the finest of cloth, corseted and hooped with the best of them. So that was what was in the parcel that was on the Chieftain's table. She looked fine indeed, but the expression on her face was one of uncertainty. As she walked toward the door, many of the girls had the urge to embrace her, but they were stopped by Dame Brittah's footmen. Morna hesitated as if she too wanted more time for goodbyes.

"Come sister, our carriage awaits us. We have an audience with Her Majesty and must not tarry any longer," Dame Brittah called to her.

Lady Morna's station was now well above theirs and they would not be allowed the intimate time to say goodbye that all of them greatly desired.

The noble women moved through the door and into the awaiting carriage.

Everyone just stood there, looking at the door in silence. It was as if they were waiting for Morna to come back in, to tell them she had changed her mind. But she did not come back in. Morna was gone.

Sara clapped her hands together to bring them back to the moment and dismissed them to return to their chores.

"Off ya go lasses, ya all have jobs to attend," her voice was a bit shaky. They all turned and quietly went about their chores.

Life in the shire continued as life always does. So many new faces had come to the tavern: Master Thomas and Lady Isabella Campbell, Mistress Meg, Mistress Fiona Ross, Maggie, and many more. All fine residents of the shire and loyal friends of the Wycked Aye.

Maitiú's brewery was doing much better and times seemed good. Philip was a regular at the tavern, reciting his verses and telling stories as he always did. He had not accompanied Katie to Skye. Clan MacAlasdair and Clan MacLeod do not get along and Philip would not be welcome there.

Maureen missed Morna terribly, as they all did and she prayed every day for Heber's return.

Two months had passed since Morna left, and more than three months since Heber's disappearance. Maureen was at the stables and was not due at the tavern for an hour or so.

It was mid-afternoon and the tavern was beginning to fill with hungry and thirsty patrons. Maitiú and Phillip were playing dice at the bar, and Fiona was moving through the tavern cleaning tables and singing a little tune as she always did, when a strapping young lad, battle hardened and weary from the road came in.

Slowly the tavern began to quiet as the folk of the Wycked Aye caught site of this lad walking toward the bar and carrying a sword.

Philip was turning the dice cup when he noticed the young lad. He stopped in the middle of his roll and dropped the dice cup to the bar.

"Ye've only had one Ale Philip and yer already droppin' the dice cup?" Maitiú poked at him. When he noticed Philip's expression, he too turned to see the young lad. Maitiú dropped his ale to the floor and barely caught himself from falling as his knees buckled underneath him.

"Dónal, Dónal me son, I can nay believe me eyes. Thanks be to God yer alive." Maitiú began to reach for his son when he realized what Dónal was carrying in his hands. Within a single beat, Maitiú's heart went from great happiness to profound sorrow for in his son's arms was the sword of Chieftain Heber MacPherson. Mistress Meg screamed out in shock and collapsed into a chair near the fire. Fiona rushed to her side. Silence filled the tavern.

Dónal took a step closer to his father and said, "He saved us Da, he saved us all. He asked me to bring this back to the Wycked Aye. None of us woulda ever left that cursed land of Morocco without Heber. The whole bloody brigade owes their lives to the MacPherson himself."

The sound of whispers and gentle sobs could be heard throughout the Wycked Aye. Maitiú took the sword from his son, held it for a moment and then passed the sword to Phillip who did the same. The sword was passed from patron to patron, many either raising the blade to their forehead or placing a kiss upon it, until it came back to Maitiú.

With sword in hand, Maitiú turned to his son and embrace him, "Welcome home son, welcome home. May God rest Heber MacPhearson."

Lady Isabella moved close to her husband as tears began to stream down her cheeks.

Oh Thomas, so it be true. This be dangerous news for the shire husband," she whispered. "Aye and fer sure when this reaches Argyle he be movin' quickly ta try and befriend Heber's alliances. What shall we do?"

"I know wife, but we must be careful," he said quietly as he consoled and comforted his wife. "No one can know who sent us here. These be good people and they have become our dear friends. It be time now ta mourn Heber MacPherson, we need to wait and be patient."

When Maureen got to the tavern, there was an uneasy weight in the air. No one was lingering outside as they often did on clear autumn days. She suddenly had a sick feeling in her belly and knew that something was terribly wrong. She hesitated at the door as if something was holding her back. She slowly placed her hand upon the door. As she pushed the door open, she immediately heard the sounds of sadness. She caught sight of Philip and saw the sword in his hands. When his eyes met hers, they told her everything she had feared for so long. She knew, she knew! Heber was dead.

Philip called out to her, "Lass wait, do nay go."

But she turned and ran out of the tavern. She ran and did not look back.

Chapter Eight

Rowan

Chestofbooks.com

Cold, so very cold. The stiffening ache in her bones raised her from a deep sleep. Maureen awoke to find herself somewhere in the forest, in the dark and alone. Panic overtook her and she scrambled to her feet, turning in circles; first right, then left until she caught her foot on a fallen branch and tumbled back to the ground.

She put her hands to her head as a screaming pain pounded beneath her skull. "What the bloody hell happened?" she thought. She remembered running from the tavern. She remembered crying as she ran toward the stables. She remembered Olaf waiting for her outside the stables and then riding away with him.

"Get a hold of yerself girl," she said to herself. "Ya've been in the forest at night before." Her head was still pounding—pounding from the uncontrolled sobbing for the loss of her Chieftain and friend.

She slowly looked around. She had no idea of how she had arrived in this place, whatever this place was. There was but little light in the sky as only a crescent moon shown in the night sky. Her eyes struggled to adjust to the darkness. She could see that she was sitting on the edge of a clearing surrounded by great trees. To the center, she could see what appeared to be another circle of large stones. Inside that was a pile of wood or maybe a small shelter next to another great tree. But it was too dark to see clearly.

Her heart jumped once more when she suddenly heard a rustling of brush behind her, and out came Olaf into the clearing, tossing his head as he came forward. Maureen rushed to him and threw her arms around his great neck.

"Oh, me dear friend, I be so glad to see ya." She held him tightly, taking in his warmth and strength. "However did ya find me here?" she asked of her hoofed companion.

"He is the one who brought you here child." Maureen snapped around to see who was speaking. She saw no one before her, but the voice was strangely familiar. She held close to Olaf, scanning the forest around her, straining her eyes to make sense of the shapes and shadows around her.

"He brought you here at my bidding." The voice was coming from the trees just behind Olaf. Maureen looked up and there, perched on a large lower branch was a being she had not seen for many moons.

She rose and stood on the branch just above her and her horse. As Maureen's eyes became more accustomed to the darkness, she could see the being more clearly. She looked much as she did when Maureen had first met her on that day out on the moors. It was Shalynn. Not but four feet tall, her willowy body was embellished with intricate markings and symbols. As before, she was clad in the wrappings of a warrior: leather leggings, wrist guards and upper body armor. Her upper arms were wrapped in silver bands and her long black hair was laced back with leather. A thin, silver headband bearing a single green gem adorned her brow. A bow and quiver were bound to her back and a stiletto hung from her belt. She was beautifully daunting.

She spoke something to Olaf in a language Maureen did not understand. He obediently stepped backwards until his hind quarters were just under the branch where she stood. She delicately stepped on to his back and walked up to his shoulders.

"A chara Shalynn of the Aes Sidhe, the honor is mine." Maureen did her best to greet Shalynn in her best Gaelic, and with respect for the being that she was. This woman had saved her life and she deserved Maureen's gratitude and respect.

"Again, we meet Little Mary. Improved your manners have become since our last meeting," she said with a bit of a chuckle. Again she spoke to Olaf and he obediently raised his front leg for her to step to the ground.

"I feel your sorrow for the loss of your Chieftain. The MacPherson was an honorable and gallant warrior. His actions saved the lives of many. He was important to you, yes?"

Suddenly tears again began to well up in Maureen's eyes and her words caught in her throat as she tried to speak, "Aye, aye that he was. Shalynn, why have ya brought me here? What be this place?"

Shalynn walked over to a large stone nearby and climbed upon it so they might speak eye-to-eye. As she turned to face Maureen, she raised her hands to the trees around them and said, "This child, is the Sacred

Circle of Rowan, a place of great power to the Aes Sidhe. I have brought you here for healing."

Maureen had heard many tales of the magic of the rowan trees. Not long ago, a group of the Highlanders had gathered for the day near a river that runs not far from the tavern. They had a fine day of games and good food, and were sharing a tankard of Maitiú's ale when he began to tell a story of the faerie trees. For just across the river there was a fairly large hill, and all the trees had been cleared except for a great oak at the very top. Maitiú told of how when men would cut the trees for building and firewood, they would always leave one tree for the faeries and that was how the faeries would travel between worlds. Had Maureen not known of the woman standing before her, she would have passed it off as a silly little tale.

Shalynn stepped down from the stone and began to walk toward the center of the circle. Maureen did not follow, as she had no intention of staying in this place much longer. She was cold, hungry and exhausted. She wanted to return to her cottage and be left alone to morn her Chieftain in silence.

When Shalynn saw her hesitation, she turned back to her and said, "Come child, your time draws near."

"What do ya mean?" Maureen began to follow her into the circle. They passed through the circle of trees and approached the inner circle of stone. Olaf had followed, but stopped when they passed the boundary of stone.

"Shalynn, we be not bloody stayin' here, are we?" Maureen's eyes had now adjusted to the darkness of the night and she could see a shelter at the base of a great rowan tree in the center of the circle. More of a hovel—a sod shelter built into the tree.

"No child. We are not staying here. Only you are," she replied.

"Yer leavin' me here, alone?" Maureen was more angry than frightened. But in her heart, she knew that Shalynn only appeared when she was in great need. She was a protector—a guardian—and would not put her in danger. They had reached the entrance to the hovel at the base of the great rowan.

"In this shelter you will find food, drink, warmth and safety. It is time to rest Little Mary, and heal. At dawn, a friend and a Sheppard of the Forest will meet you and see you home." In the blink of an eye, she was again perched on a lower limb of the great tree.

"Good journey to you child; we will meet again." And then she was gone.

"Gone, she be bloody arse gone. Leavin' me stuck in the middle of fookin' nowhere and this was supposed to be some kind of healing?" Maureen turned and yelled up to the tree, "Bloody arse faeries!" She paced around the base of the great rowan kicking dirt and muttering to herself. Finally, frustrated, exhausted and out of foul words to express her anger, she just stopped and tears again began to fall. She dropped to the ground and put her face to her hands. How had things come to this? She had been alone most of her life. Somehow, she had managed to make her own way. She had been close to no one and no one had been close to her. All she had to worry about was herself. Then she wandered into that damn tavern. She found Katie, who became the sister she never had, and then Katie left. She came to trust and depend on Fionnula, and then Fionnula left. She had turned to

Morna, and now Morna had gone away as well.

But most of all, she had come to love Heber. He took her in and showed her kindness as no one else had ever done, and now he was dead.

Maureen was chilled all the way to the bone. The height of night was nearing and true darkness had engulfed the sacred circle. Her clothes were beginning to dampen from the mist rising from the forest floor. She looked back to the great tree and moved closer to it so that she might place her hands to its trunk.

"I thank ya for the protection of this circle, and for the warmth and shelter ya offer me this night. I have heard the old women of the Highlands call ya the Travelers Tree. They say ya protect the wayward traveler from bein' lost. Tell me rowan, can ya show me a path for me heart to follow? For right now, great rowan, it be truly lost."

She was exhausted and in need of rest. She turned her attention to the hovel. There appeared to be a faint glow coming from inside and she could feel warmth as she approached the doorway. The comforting scent of a turf fire touched her senses and beckoned her in. She half expected to see her mum standing over a cook pot after a long day of tending the flock. As she entered the hovel, the opening behind her disappeared and sealed her inside for the night.

This was not a hovel at all; this a faerie mound. When the doorway closed behind her, she was startled, but not frightened. In fact, she felt quite safe.

As Shalynn had promised, a table sat near the fire and upon it lay a platter of dried meat, fruit, some oat cakes and what appeared to be a pitcher of country wine. A platform placed to the side of the mound was topped with a feather bed, and upon it was a clean, white linen chemise.

Maureen felt as if she could stay here forever. The mound had a faint glow inside, much like the light that had surrounded Shalynn the first time Maureen had met her. The walls were alive with ferns and flowers, and the fire burned brightly in a small stone hearth. She changed from her damp clothes into the chemise and placed her skirts by the fire to dry.

The food was most welcome and quite satisfying. She poured a mug of wine and pulled her chair closer to the fire. The pounding in her head had subsided and every muscle in her body seemed relaxed.

After a few sips of wine, she realized this was no ordinary mead, this was rowan berry wine. The Highlanders often made wine from the red berries of the rowan trees and it was known to be a potent concoction. She had heard the old women tell tales of this mixture as well. They said it gave its drinker the power of sight, particularly the women of Skye. Maureen did not care about the tales. The wine was soothing and put her body at ease. It did not take long for the wine to take effect. She lay down on the bed and allowed herself to drift into a most needed and very deep sleep.

She awoke to the scent of lavender and the sweet sound of a delicate voice softly singing an Irish lullaby.

"Well, it be about time. I be sorry to wake ya from yer sleep daughter, but me time here be short."

Dear God in Heaven, how could this be? She looked so beautiful, as she did when she was young. Maureen slowly raised up from the bed and sat on the edge to face her.

"Mum? I can nay believe me eyes. How can this be?

Be it truly you?" Maureen whispered to her.

"Aye...and nay," she replied.

"What are ya doin' here Mum, how did ya get here?"

"Shalynn summoned me. Ya know, sometimes a lass just needs to talk to her Mum." She reached forward and pushed Maureen's hair back away from her face in that soft, gentle way that mothers do. Maureen reached up to touch her hand, it was soft and warm, just as she remembered.

"Tell me, why do ya run from the folk who care about ya, Little Mary? They be yer family now, they care for ya, can ya nay see that child?"

Maureen could feel the tears begin again. She tried to look at her, but she could not meet her gaze.

Her mum cupped Maureen's chin in her hand and raised her eyes to hers. She did not speak, but her brow rose slightly in that way that women do, waiting for Maureen to explain herself.

"It just seems like everything be bloody fallin' apart. As soon as I start to care about someone, they either leave or they die. Times be so hard now, so hard for so many. I spend so much time at chapel praying that Father Desmond has started to make me leave and go..."

"Home, he sends you home to the Wycked Aye does he not?"

Maureen looked at her in amazement. She was right. It was what he said every time he offered her a hand up from the prayer bench. 'Go on home now, Maureen, back to the Wycked Aye,' he would say.

Maureen's mother saw the realization in her daughter's eyes and Maureen saw a slight smile cross her loving face.

"Ya see child, ya had the answer all along. Yer just so damn stubborn, ya wouldna let anyone help ya find it." She looked toward the fire as if listening to something. She placed both her hands-on Maureen's face and said, "Time runs short, I must go now me daughter. Yer time here comes to an end as well. It passes very quickly inside the mounds. This be not me world and it nay be yers as well. The faerie mounds exist in between the realms of the living and those who have crossed." She rose and began to turn toward the fire.

"I wish we had more time," Maureen whispered to her. "There be so much I want to share with ya, so much has happened." Her mind raced over her life since her mother had passed. Wenching through taverns in the Lowlands to get by, Armstrong, her father's death—so much to account for.

As her mother turned back to Maureen her image began to change. She was fading away right before Maureen's eyes.

"Ah lass, the past be behind ya," she said. "There be not a thing ya can do to change that which has already come to pass. So 'twould be best to make peace with it now and just let it go. As fer what be down the road, well, only the gifted are given a glimpse of that. Not even we can see what the future holds. Our time here together runs short Little Mary. I must return to me world and ya must return to yers. I leave ya with this me child: those who pass over are never truly gone. Hold those ya love close to yer heart and they will always be with ya. Walk yer path as ya will, harm not a thing as ya go, and do yer best to stay within God's good graces. We will meet again me daughter. Until then, trust in the goodly folk of the Wycked Aye.

They are true friends and they need ya, just as much as you need them. As Shalynn has told ya, ya be one of the chosen Irish and the daughter of a MacLeod. Whatever gifts God has granted to ya child, I pray ya use them most wisely."

She turned and began to walk toward the fire. Maureen wanted to run to her and hold her with her forever, but she knew that was not to be. Her mother stepped into the flames and vanished leaving behind the sweet scent of lavender.

Maureen changed from the chemise back into her skirts and bodice. She poured herself a mug of rowan berry wine and sat down next to the fire. A large bowl of water sat upon the table with some rowan leaves floating on top. Curious, as she had not notice them when she first entered the mound. As she looked at the bowl, the leaves began to float around in a circle. Around and around they went until they floated to the edge of the bowl leaving the center of the water clear. As she looked into the water, she could not believe what her eyes beheld.

Heber? Heber? Could it be? And then the image was gone. She did not know what to think. She looked into her cup of wine and thought, I did nay have that much, did I?

Just as the door to the mound had closed, it slowly began to open. Maureen's time there was done. She walked outside to see the great rowan before her, its leaves and flowers shining in the morning sun. She wrapped her arms around the trunk of the tree.

"Me thanks to ya great rowan and to you, Shalynn of the Aes Sidhe."

She heard the familiar sound of her dear Olaf and she turned to see her beloved stallion standing in the outer circle of trees, with him stood the Warrior- Poet and the Irishman.

"Good marrow me friends," she shouted and ran up the path toward them.

"Philip, how did you find me?"

"Oh, a little Faerie told me," he replied jokingly.

Maitiú embraced her, "Are ya alright lass?"

She put her hands on his shoulders, put him at arm's length and said, "Oh Maitiú, our Heber is gone and me heart is heavy with sorrow. But I know now where I belong and where me path will lead me. Come on lads, follow me. I be buyin' ya both an ale and we will drink to our Chieftain."

"But ya do nay even know where ya be goin'," he said.

"Aye, but I do know," she said as she picked up Olaf's reins. "This be me path and it leads straight to the Wycked Aye."

Philip looked back to the great rowan and just grinned.

Chapter Nine

Búiochas do Dhia!

Tribal-Celtic-Tattoos

Maitiú was filled with a general sense of melancholy. There was change everywhere and change was always difficult, especially for Maitiú. There was an old saying that read: There is one thing in life that consistently remains the same— that everything changes.

Father Brian counseled Maitiú, "Remember, when God closes one door, He opens another."

"But Father, what if you do nay like what be behind the new door?"

"Maitiú, when we suffer change, the little deaths in our lives, we must trust that God will guide us ta something new and better."

That was it then, trust in God. Maitiú trusted God would see him through eventually but it did not seem to make the here and now less painful.

"God be pruning the branches so they may bear more fruit," Maitiú thought.

More than he cared to admit, the pain of losing his friend Heber weighed heavily on him. It weighed heavily on Maureen as well. There was the sad correspondence from the Earldom of the misfortunes of Earl Gerald in his dealings with the English crown. There was the rumor of Argyll buying the brewery from Earl Gerald. Argyll! Lord Earl Argyll, Archibald Campbell, who hated everything about Maitiú except the taste of his ale.

Lastly, there was the less than cordial welcome he was beginning to receive from the new proprietor of the Wycked Aye, Sara MacBride. If it was not for Maureen and Philip, and the long-term contract between the brewery and the tavern, Maitiú was sure he would receive no welcome at all.

As was his new practice, Maitiú spent more time at his desk in the brewery. It was there he kept his books with his debts, credits, resources and problems. Keeping the books was a dark, dreary, but necessary task. He wondered why the bookkeeping task never changed. There was the changing of ale recipes driven by the ever-changing supply of grains and hops. That could be fun—it was creative. But the joy was taken out of it with deadlines and the urgency of contracts.

So, one overcast, windy day where it had been pissing rain on and off, a dark-haired, dusky complexioned foreigner came knocking around the brewery. By his vigor and martial bearing, Maitiú' figured it was one of his son's comrades from the Papal Army, maybe even an officer.

Upon greeting one another, they spent the next few minutes trying to converse. Maitiú and the officer finally settled on a combination of Church Latin, broken English, broken German and lots of hand gestures. Neither conversant spoke in their first language, but Maitiú' gleaned from this stubble of words that the man did serve with the Papal Army, he was interested in seeing Dónal, but more importantly, he had something important to give to Maitiú. Out of his pocket he pulled on object carefully wrapped in lightly oiled leather. It was a MacPherson clan badge. There was writing on the leather. It was smudged and illegible, but it looked like Heber's hand had written it. Was it another memento? Dónal brought home his sword, so now Maitiú had his clan badge? He bid his guest sit down. Maitiú called out to his assistant, "Hamish, give this man all he wants for ale and food. I need to find Dónal, Meg MacPherson and Maureen." He flew out the door in haste leaving Hamish with the foreigner. They could only communicate via an ale glass, yet it was a lively conversation.

Finding Dónal was easy. Since his return from Morocco, he spent most of his waking hours in the chapel. When he was not on his knees before the Blessed Sacrament, he was helping Father Brian with maintaining it and serving at the Mass.

Maureen was either at the stables or in the tavern. Maitiú sought her first in the Wycked Aye where he found her.

Philip greeted Maitiú, "Hello stranger, Ta' fa'ilte romhat."

"Philip, go fetch Dónal from the Chapel and meet us at the brewery. De'an deifer!"

"Ta' go maith, boyo, I'll hurry, but I'll be expectin' an explanation later."

Hurrying behind the bar and into the backroom

Maitiú' found her. "A Maureen, a sto'r, come quickly, to the brewery, anois!" Seeing the urgency in his eyes, Maureen doffed her apron, donned her cape and headed with Maitiú for the door. Sara saw them before they got outside.

"Where are ya off to lass? Who be coverin' yer work?" Sara looked first at Maureen and then her eyes met the Irishman's. That look prompted her to say, "Go then, but come back promptly or ya be getting' no wages for the day." Sara, in frustration, turned and said, "Who be coverin' her work?" An older woman in a dark shawl walked in from the doorway and said to Sara, "I be a friend of Maureen's. We met in the woods a while back. I be coverin' her work."

"Well I thank ya M'lady. Maureen be blessed to have such a friend."

Meg was nowhere to be found. As Maureen and Maitiú' approached the brewery office they saw Dónal and Philip walking toward the brewery. The four of them entered at once and found the foreigner in an ale induced fog. When Dónal saw the foreigner, he snapped to attention. Then, in Italian, Dónal said, "Captain Mario Rossi!" When Rossi saw Dónal the ale-induced fog lifted and he jumped up and embraced Dónal. The two battle-hardened soldiers shook hands and wept for at least half a minute.

Mario and Dónal babbled for the next five minutes. Tears were pouring down both of their cheeks. Maureen's patience finally ran out and she exclaimed, "For the love of Christ, Dónal, what he be sayin'?"

"That Heber MacPherson be alive!"

Maitiú' called out loudly to Hamish, who was only a few paces away, "Hamish, lad, bring out the special reserve, that Rhineland lager. Dónal and Mario have a story to tell."

Two quaffs of the lager were enough to loosen Dónal's tongue and he began to describe his version of the final battle with the Moors.

"We were drawn out of the safety of our fort by the taunts of Moorish footmen and archers. Lord Cardoso, our Portuguese commander, lost his composure and wanted to attack. Heber and Mario advised against it. Heber told the Cardoso these footmen reminded him of the bogtrotting Irish—sorry Da—who taunted the English out of formation and then destroyed them in detail in a running battle. Cardoso brushed aside Heber's concerns. He was as fearless as he was foolish.

We formed up in a column and marched out. We went out, commanded by Heber and were first over a small set of rocky hills that opened up into a wide valley. As we crossed the valley in pursuit of the Moorish footmen, we suddenly saw horsemen in the distance. There were so many and they came at great speed. I shot one rider, but the rest rushed past me as if I was of no consequence. Heber formed the men up in a square. The pikes and halberds jutted out from the formation like the quills on a hedgehog. Formation intact, they began a slow retreat back to the rocky hills. At first the horsemen flew into our lads, but horse and rider were hurled back in bloody pieces. The Moorish cavalry then circled the square and their mounted archers fired arrows. Our ranks began to whittle away. It was soon I was able to rejoin the formation, as I was partially hidden in the dust and confusion.

We Irish boys always kept darts about us and were able to knock down some riders, but it was not enough. We almost made it out of the valley when we ran into our own van. They were in route and fleeing in panic. Officers screamed orders and counter orders, but the calm and steady voice of MacPherson speaking in Gaelic kept us Irish boys intact. When we finally made it into the rocks, we formed a perimeter with rocks and bodies while dodging arrows. Many of us were grievously wounded and the night was beginning to fall.

The Moors pulled back now, content to let us bleed and shiver in the cold night of the desert. The morning and our end would come soon enough. That's when Captain Heber called me out to run for help. He said, 'give me that Irish toothpick you're carrying and let me give you a real sword.' He handed me his sword and said quietly, 'If help cannot be had, bring my sword back to your Da'.' I did nay want to leave, but I was the fastest runner and could run forever, just like me Da. So off in the darkness I fled. Once through the Moorish picket line, I saw the remains of our rearguard and knew all was lost. Some Moors occupied the fort as they undoubtedly overwhelmed the garrison. On through the night I fled and when I reached port, I told the ship's captain what had transpired. We weighed anchor and left with the tide."

Looking toward Mario, the Italian took over the story with Dónal translating.

"Some of us from the van hid in the rocks. Most of us were wounded as well. From there we saw at dawn's first light the attack that ended our company. It had taken about as long as it takes a fat man to eat his breakfast. The Moors ran off with our banner, yipping like roosters with burning tail feathers. The looters and Moorish camp followers came in to strip and rob the dead, and murder the wounded.

Among the looters was a Turk, a Saracen. They are the mercenaries of the Turkish Calif. Most were once Christian boys pressed into service at a very young age. This Saracen had a physician in his company. They were looking for wounded men for the physician to practice on.

The physician was like a barber-surgeon, bonesetter and apothecary rolled into one. Apparently, he needed training on his barber-surgeon skills. If he killed any of us it wouldn't matter.

They gathered about a dozen of us in a tent. I saw MacPherson, my fellow captain, lying there on a cot. He looked as if he had been clubbed. He appeared as dead when the physician took an awl and scored a hole in his head. I thought it was some sort of heathen torture, but a day later Heber was awake and, in a week, he was up and walking around. His Italian was horrible, but it was never that good even before." At that point Philip snickered and begged Mario to continue with a hand gesture.

"The Saracen kept us in a tent for a month. He told me in perfect Italian that he had once been a Christian boy from Dalmatia and hoped one of us would return to his village and tell his family he still lived. He brought us back on a ship to Constantinople. I convince the Saracen I knew where his village was so he released me. Before I left, MacPherson snuck his badge into my hands. He had somehow kept it away from our captors."

At that point in the story Dónal noticed his father's face in a wide grin and Maureen weeping with joy. Sobbing, Maureen said, "He lives, he lives, Bui'ochas do Dhia." Then turning abruptly to Maitiú' and Philip she asked, "Now, how do we get him back?"

As if on cue, Meg MacPherson strode into the brewery office. She undoubtedly heard the tail-end of the conversation.

"Clan Chattan will find a way. We be bringin' Heber home!"

Chapter Ten

The Company

Hamish, Dónal and Captain Rossi had all fallen into a drunken slumber on the brewery office floor. Mistress Meg, Phillip, Maitiú and Maureen continued their discussion as to how they would proceed with such a task as bringing Heber home. It was decided that, for now, they would not share Captain Rossi's news of Heber with the others at the tavern. He was alive when Rossi left him, but they did not know if that would be the case when they found him. It would not be right to give false hopes to so many who missed Heber so much.

"Come Maureen, ya need to be getting back to the tavern. Sara will be mad as a hornet if ya do nay return soon, and I need to make arrangements for me journey," said Meg.

"Journey, what do ya mean Mistress?" asked Maureen.

"Lass, raising a company for an expedition such as this will take money, money we presently do nay have," she replied. Little did she know that sitting in Heber's private cash keep at the tavern sat a bag full of gold, Maureen's bag of fifty gold sovereign; enough to buy an army and a ship of their own. Maureen felt badly that she was going off on a long and difficult trip when the money she needed was right here. Yet Maureen knew that money could never be used or told of to anyone. That bag of gold had been kept at the tavern and the bag of gemstones had been well hidden at Castle Elliot since Maureen's return from the border. Only Heber, Lord Cullen and she knew of them, and there they must remain for now.

Maureen asked, "Well, where will ya go Meg?"

"To Badenoch, I be seekin' an audience with the leaders of Clan Chattan and askin' for the funds for our campaign."

"We be goin' with ya Meg," offered Maitiú.

"Aye, that we will," chimed Philip.

"I be most grateful to ya lads. But neither one of ya would be welcome in the halls of Clan Chattan. But do nay worry, I will nay be goin' alone. Come Maureen, it be gettin' late, we need to be on our way, and I believe you two lads have two soldiers and a brewery keep to put to bed," she said. They looked over at the three men heaped on the brewery floor sound asleep.

"What say ya Philip, shall we put them to bed or leave them where they be?"

"They already be on the floor. Leave them be, they can nay fall any farther," Phillip chuckled.

Meg looked back to Maitiú, "Oh and Maitiú, when the men come around, please ask the Italian to stay on as me guest. We be needin' him as part of the company. Let him know he'll be well paid." Maitiú nodded his head acknowledging Meg's request.

He admired the strength and courage of Meg MacPherson, but wondered if she fully realized the gravity of the task that lay before them. It would take near a month's time for the journey to Badenoch and back. The company would then need to be assembled and the real task would begin. A voyage to the Ottoman Empire, halfway across the world it seemed. But he had faith in Meg all the same. She was a Highlander woman and she was Heber's kin; determined and courageous. If it meant bringing Heber home alive, she would see this journey through to the end. As she left the brewery office, he said to himself, "Christ be with you Meg, and with Heber. May God help us all."

As they left the brewery office, the storm that had been threatening off-and-on all morning had finally settled in and the rain was falling steadily. Maureen donned her cloak and made a mad dash for the tavern. Mistress Meg headed into the shire on errands. As Maureen jogged down the pathway, the roads were getting muddy and puddles were filling up everywhere. She was wet and cold but her heart was full of warmth and happiness. For now, there was hope, hope that they would find Heber and bring him home.

She knew it. She knew it all along. That night in the mound at the base of the great rowan, she had seen him in the water. She had seen him. She remembered her mother's words, 'whatever gifts God has given to ya child, use them wisely.' Her night in the mound between the worlds of men and Fey had awakened a gift, a gift known to the

MacLeod women of Skye. She had the sight, she could see. She could see!

She began laughing out loud, spinning in circles in the rain, jumping into puddles and kicking the water like a child. By the time she reached the tavern, her boots were covered in mud and she was drenched to the bone. She flew through the door to the tavern and ran straight into Chieftain Sara.

"It be about bloody time!" she exclaimed.

Oh shite, she was in for it now.

"Me apologies Sara, I lost track of time."

"Yer always losing track of time. Every time you walk out that door with that Irishman you lose track of time. Ya be staying extra hours tonight to make up for it." Her voice was stern, but her words were not spoken in anger.

"Why are ya smilin' like that lass, are ya mockin' me?"

Maureen had not realized that her face was, in fact, one big smile from ear to ear. She wanted so much to tell her—she wanted to tell everyone. She wanted to jump on a table and shout "Heber be alive!" But she could not.

"Oh, not at all Chieftain, not at all, I be stayin' as long as ya need me," she said, wiping the smile from her face.

"Now get yer apron and get to work girl," Sara extended her arm and pointed Maureen to the pantry.

"Aye Sara, as you wish." As she turned away, the smile returned to her face. She hurried back to the pantry to hang up her wet cloak and get her apron.

"Ya best be stayin' out of the Chieftain's way tonight lass." It was Isabella. "She be none too happy with ya. If it had nay been for yer friend coverin' for ya, ya'd be getting' no wages for the day. Ya can nay be runnin' off with that Irishman every time he comes into the tavern.

"I know Tánaiste, I be truly sorry. But it was important and…hold on, what friend?"

"The woman from the forest, she left just before ya got back."

"But I do nay know anyone from…what was her name?"

"Do nay believe she gave us her name, said to give ya her wages. Sara sent her on her way with some bread and cheese for her work. Now get yerself out there and get to it. Goin' to be a long night."

And a long night it was. The tavern was full to the brim with travelers taking shelter from the rain.

The time flew by. Maureen felt like she had energy enough for three. Phillip, Maitiú, Dónal, Captain Rossi and Hamish all came in for supper. When they entered the tavern, everyone turned to look at the dark-skinned foreigner. Chieftain Sara caught sight of them and gave Maitiú a stern glance. She motioned them to a table in back, out of the way.

When Maureen saw them come in, she grabbed her tray, a basket of brown bread and headed for their table.

Sara stopped her on the way, "Do nay let me see ya sittin' or carousin' at that table, ya hear me now?"

"I hear ya, loud and clear," Maureen replied. "No sittin' or carousin'." When she reached the table, she served them the bread. "Good evenin' gents."

"Good evenin' Mistress MacLeod. Pull a chair and join us," said Dónal.

"I be afraid I can nay join ya tonight Dónal. Chieftain has made it quite clear there be no sittin' or carousin' this night. Now, what can I get ya, ales all around or have ya had yer fill for today?"

Maureen noticed, for as inebriated as they had been earlier in the day, Rossi and Dónal seemed to be doing well. Hamish, however, was looking a bit pale and unsettled. Three ales were ordered for Philip, Maitiú and Dónal. Hamish asked for tea. Maureen turned to the Italian, "Vino, per favore signora giovane," he said. She looked at Dónal.

"Wine Maureen, he would like some wine." She bowed her head to him, then he reached around and promptly slapped her on her backside. She screamed and stepped back from the table. Captain Rossi seemed confused by her response. Dónal leaned over and whispered to Rossi that such attentions might be acceptable in Rome, but not in the Scottish Highlands. Philip and Maitiú just laughed.

Maureen brought the ales and wine, and a full plate of pork, cabbage and potatoes. All poor Hamish could manage was some broth and bread.

It was not until the wee hours that Maureen returned to her cottage. She placed the lantern she was carrying on the table and there, sitting on the table was a small round of bread, a wedge of cheese and a small branch from a rowan tree. She shook her head, "Shalynn, bloody arse faeries."

When Meg MacPherson left the brewery, she headed straight to the Couriers office at the stables to arrange for messengers on the following day. She needed riders to carry three missives: one to Collin

Macintosh, the Chief of Clan Chattan; one to Robert MacPherson, head of Clan MacPherson; and the last to her nephew, Faolan Mackintosh, who she would ask to be her escort for the long journey to Badenoch.

She had not seen her nephew for quite some time, but knew he was in the employ of a nobleman named Hamilton near Edinburgh. Faolan's mother, Meg's sister, had passed when Faolan was young. Faolan's father was a merchant sailor and was often gone to sea for long periods of time. Meg had helped see to the lad while he was young. He had grown into a fine, hard-working young man. He moved around a lot, but he always managed to get a message to Meg to let her know where he was and that he was alright.

When Meg entered the Courier's office, Mr. Macaulay looked up with great surprise.

"Good Lord Mistress Meg, what would ya be doin' out on a day like this? Ya should be back at the Wycked Aye sittin' by a warm fire!"

"I can nay agree with ya more Master Macaulay, but I must speak with ya on a matter of great urgency. I need two riders to carry messages to Badenoch and Edinburgh on the marrow."

When Seán Macaulay heard the intensity in Meg's voice, he put his joviality aside.

"I be sorry Meg, but I have only one rider in at present. The other two are out, and their return has been delayed by the storm."

When Meg heard this, she sighed in exasperation. She placed her hands on the counter and dropped her head. She did not need delays of any kind; every moment lost was a moment longer away from Heber.

Seán Macaulay was a large, burley man, a true Gael; strong as an ox and gentle as a lamb. His heart was as big as he was. He placed his hands upon Meg's and said, "I be tellin' ya what, ya have those missives to me on the marrow, and I be findin' ya yer riders." Meg raised her eyes to meet his. She could see the concern in his face.

"Yer an angel Seán Macaulay, that be what ya arc." Shc placed her hands on his cheeks and pulled him toward her and placed a kiss on his forehead.

"God love ya Seán." Then she turned and hurried back out into the storm.

Meg did not return to the tavern when she left Mr. Macaulay's office. She went home to her cottage and set to writing her missives that would put the wheels in motion to bring Heber home. She was almost done with the second missive when a chill ran through her bones and she realized she was cold and hungry. She had been at the brewery since mid-day. She was so consumed by the task before her she had failed to take food or drink.

When she arrived at her cottage, she had forgotten to build a fire. She was not thinking clearly, her mind was not where it should be. In one day, she had news that Heber was still alive and had committed herself to the task of raising a company and bringing him home. The task seemed monumental, but she knew she must see it through.

She moved to the hearth and laid the makings of a fire. She struck a spark to the tinder and watched as the small flames grew into a warm blaze. She wrapped a shawl around her shoulder and returned to her writing. When the ink had dried, she folded and wax sealed the missives with the signet of Clan

MacPherson. The first step was done. Now she must wait, wait for Faolan to arrive at the tavern. Together they would make the journey north to Badenoch. It would be at least ten days before Faolan would arrive from Edinburgh. That should give her time to make an excuse for her absence from the tavern with Chieftain Sara, and prepare their supplies for the journey. But for now, what she mostly needed was a bite of food and some rest.

The rain had passed and Maureen awoke to a cold, clear morning. She had little time to waste, as the farrier was coming to the tavern stables to trim the horse's hoofs and shoe them. She quickly dressed and took advantage of the bread and cheese left on her table for a quick breakfast. The branch from the rowan tree had two nice bunches of berries attached. She grabbed them up and headed out the door, nibbling on sweet rowan berries as she walked to the stables. Olaf was waiting in his stall for his morning carrot, as was Maitiú's two Connemara ponies, Hope and Grace.

"Good morning girls," she said as she gave them their treat. Olaf grumbled in his stall and tossed his head, "Ladies first mister, wait yer turn." She got to work, for she had four stalls to clean and four horses to feed before William arrived.

William Macaulay was the farrier and the son of Seán Macaulay. He was a good-sized man, like his father, with long, dark hair and grey-blue eyes. He was indeed a fine sight to behold. William cared for his father's horses and helped out at the blacksmith.

He also rode as a courier when his father needed his help.

Maureen had all the stalls cleaned, but only two of the horses fed and brushed when William arrived.

"Good marrow Maureen."

"William, ya be early."

"Aye, my apologies to ya. I need to get started early as I be ridin' out this afternoon," he said. He put down his tool bucket and walked back to Hope's stall. He gave the pony a pat on her rump, "Ready for a trim missy," he said. His shoulders were as high as the horse's.

Maureen finished giving Hope her mound of hay and ducked under her neck to speak with William. She had known him for over a year now, but the sight of him still pulled the air from her chest and the strength from her knees.

"If ya could start with Heber's stallion, and then Olaf, I be finishin' with the girls. That way I will nay be keepin' ya waiting around for nothin'."

"Well, that sounds like a plan lass." He gave Hope another pat and walked back down to the first stall. She watched him walk away, then composed herself and got on with her chores. They worked in silence for about an hour or so, William had moved on to Olaf's stall and Maureen was finished with Hope and Grace. She walked down and put her tools back in the shed. She grabbed her branch of rowan berries from the table in the tack room and went back out to visit with William. She climbed up and sat on the fence rail next to the rain barrels. The barrels were full to brim from the storm the night before. She took a rowan berry and tossed it at William. He turned to look at her. She offered him some berries, but he declined.

"So, where ya be ridin' off to William?" she asked.

"Oh, Mistress Meg dropped three missives off with me Da this morning. Michael left right away for Badenoch and I be off to Edinburgh."

"Edinburgh?" Maureen was confused. Why would Meg be sending someone to Edinburgh? She said she was heading to Badenoch to raise the funds for the company, not Edinburgh.

"Well, who would the missive be for William?"

"Her nephew, Faolan Macintosh. Seems he be in the employ of a nobleman named Hamilton. His lands are just south of Edinburgh."

Faolan, she had sent for Faolan. Faolan had left the shire not long after Maureen's return from the border, and they had not seen him since. He had been gone for such a long time it seemed. This was wonderful news, she liked Faolan very much. They had been friends from the first time they met. There was something different about Faolan. He pulled at her in a way she did not understand. Was Meg bringing him here to be part of the company or to go with her to Badenoch?

Her mind was wandering as she leaned back against the fence post and began to swirl the rowan branch through the water in the rain barrel. William was still speaking but she did not hear anything he was saying. She pulled the branch from the rain barrel, but the water continued to spin. The rowan berries. She watched intently as the water continued to spin and then slowly began to clear. She waited, hoping to see Heber—where he was, if he was safe, anything that could help the company on their journey. There was an image, she saw the sea and a shoreline. She stared into the barrel. There was a castle and standing before the castle was...dear God...Katie, Katie MacLeod. Her hand was outstretched as if she was reaching for something and...

"Maureen, Maureen! Are ya alright?"

She turned to look at William. "Are ya alright?" he repeated.

"Aye, aye I be fine. I be sorry William." When she looked back to the barrel, the image was gone.

"Did ya hear me lass?"

"No, I be sorry William, what were ya sayin'?"

"That I will nay be able to finish the fillies today. I be sendin' Patrick back on the marrow to finish up."

"Of course," she paused. "That...that be fine William, thank ya."

"Are ya sure yer alright? Ya shouldna be eatin' too many of those rowan berries. They play tricks on yer mind ya know."

He took her hand. She hopped down off the fence and brushed down her skirts.

"I will try and remember that," she said.

He walked with her to the tack room where she opened the small cashbox and paid him for his services.

"Many thanks William and have a safe trip to Edinburgh." He tossed the coins in his hand, "That I'll do lass, good day." He gathered his tools and headed back to the shire.

Maureen walked over to Olaf and put her fingers in his thick mane. "Well, what do ya make of all this me friend?" He tossed his head and neighed. She patted him on his neck and said, "I couldna agree more."

For the next few days, Maureen, Meg and the lads all went about their daily routines. No one made any reference to the company or the fact that Heber may still be alive. Meg had arranged for her time away from the tavern with Sara on the premise of family business.

Maureen said nothing to anyone about her vision of Katie in the rain barrel. Times were such that sharing something like that would get you thrown in a loch with a rock tied to your feet.

On the ninth day following the departure of the riders with Meg's missives, they were all at the tavern working as usual. Maureen could hardly wait for Faolan to arrive from Edinburgh. She cornered Meg at the bar when no one else was around.

"So, are ya all ready to head north?" She was leaning on her elbows on the bar, while Meg was behind the bar stacking tankards.

"Aye, I am. I be ridin' out on the marrow."

On the marrow, but how could she be leaving on the marrow with no escort? Maureen was beginning to wonder if Faolan was coming or not.

"But Meg, ya can nay go off by yerself. It be far too long a journey for a woman alone." She did not answer. She just looked at Maureen and smiled.

The next thing Maureen knew, two arms wrapped around her and a voice said, "Not to worry lass, she will nay be goin' alone."

She knew that voice, she knew the hands that rested on the bar next to hers and she knew the body pressed up against her. Faolan was home.

Maureen turned to face him and he put his arms around her waist and pulled her close, "Welcome home Faolan, I've missed ya."

"I've missed ya too lass, it be good to be back at the Wycked Aye." Faolan still had his arms around her when Master Thomas came up next to Meg.

"Now, now you two. We be havin' none of that. Wife!" he called to Isabella. She poked her head out from around the corner in the pantry to see what he wanted.

"Ya be needin' ta chaperon these two from now on." She just shook her head and gave him a dismissing wave of her hand. Master Thomas drew Faolan an ale. Faolan picked Maureen up by the waist, moved her to his side and picked up his ale.

"Can we sit and talk for a bit?" she asked.

"That we can, but not for too long." He lowered his voice, "Meg and I need to finish gettin' ready to leave on the marrow. Come." He took her hand and led her to a table away from the rest of the crowd.

Maureen's excitement at Faolan's return was quickly extinguished by the realization that he would be leaving the next day. They talked for about an hour or so, and then were forced to say their goodbyes. Faolan and Meg left the tavern to prepare for their departure the next day.

As they left the tavern, Fiona brushed by Maureen and gave her a poke with her elbow, "Now that be a fine one, do nay be lettin' him get away lass," she chuckled.

Maureen smiled back at her, for a fine one he was indeed. But now he was going away and would not return for a month's time. Then, he would either be on the ship with the company to retrieve Heber, or on his way back to Edinburgh. No matter the path, their time together would be short. She stood at the door of the tavern and watched them walk away. She dropped her head in disappointment. It had been so long since she had seen Faolan, and now there was so little time before he would, once again, be gone.

Maitiú and Philip had been sitting at their regular table watching the interaction between Faolan and Maureen.

"I do nay like it Maitiú, nothin' good can come of this."

"I agree Philip. I thought she had lost interest, but I see now that be not the case."

"Do you want to tell her or should I?" asked Philip.

"Nay, he be leavin' on the marrow, we be lettin' it be for now. But we can nay let this go much farther."

Philip got up and walked toward the door of the tavern. As he walked across the tavern floor, he thought about Katie. It would be good to have Katie home from Skye. He missed her terribly and needed her at times like this. Katie would be able to talk sense to Maureen, the girl would listen to Katie. Whether she would listen to him or Maitiú would remain to be seen.

Philip came up to her at the door and put his arm around her shoulders in a very fatherly manner. "I wouldna be settin' me heart on that one lass. The boy be a wanderer, he never be settlin' down. Come on now, close the door and let me buy ya a mead."

154

Master Thomas and Isabella were behind the bar.

"A glass of mead for the lass if ya please Master Thomas," requested Philip.

"As ya wish, a little mead to ease a broken heart, eh? Ah, 'tis how the world goes around lass, lovers come and lovers go. Too bad ya did nay have time for a littlc..."

"Thomas!" Isabella interjected and gave him a stern glance.

"What? I was just goin' to say that..."

"Thomas!!" She tightened her gaze.

"Aye, well...I just be goin' now to check on the fire...and the lamb. That be what I be doin'...checkin' on the fire and the lamb." He rolled his eyes at Philip and left. Isabella put her hands-on Maureen's. "Have yer drink with yer friends, lass, and then head on home for the day. The tavern be slow and we can manage just fine."

Maureen sipped her mead and talked with Maitiú and Philip about the days to come, the success of the company and the quest for Heber. They left the tavern together and she headed home alone.

The next morning Maitiú, Philip, Dónal, Captain Rossi and Maureen all met at the tavern stables to see Meg and Faolan off and wish them good journey. Faolan would be riding Heber's stallion. He was a spirited beast, a bit too spirited for Meg to handle, but Faolan would be fine. Faolan's horse would be hitched to a small cart for Meg to drive. They all helped load the cart with supplies, and saddled and hitched the horses. It was almost time for them to leave. Maureen grabbed Faolan by the shirt and pulled him back into the stable next to Olaf's stall. She wanted a few moments alone with him. They leaned up against the rail of Olaf's 'stall. She put her hands on his waist and pulled him closer.

"Have a safe trip, I be waitin' when ya get back," Maureen whispered. As he leaned forward to kiss her, Olaf turned his head and pushed Faolan out of the way.

"Olaf! What are ya doin'?" Maureen snapped.

"Looks to me like the other man in yer life be a bit jealous." Before they could move out of Olaf's reach, Meg called out.

"Faolan, it be time ta go." He quickly cupped her face in his hands and kissed her on the forehead.

"Do nay worry, there be another time." Then he turned and left.

Maureen looked at Olaf, exasperated. She had never seen him behave like that before. She put her hand in his mane and said, "Thank ya so much for that one me friend." He tossed his head and looked away.

Maureen followed Faolan out of the stable and rejoined the group. They watched as Meg and Faolan headed out on the first part of a very long journey.

The success of the company now rested solely in the hands of Meg MacPherson. For only upon her return would they know if she had the funds and support to complete the expedition, and bring Heber home.

Chapter Eleven

Tá Fáilte Romhat Arís, A Chara
(Welcome Home My Friend)

Brittish-towns.net

Meg MacPherson was as resourceful as she claimed. In less than a month, she returned from Badenoch on Spey with ten gold sovereigns and the authority to hire the company that would bring Heber MacPherson home from the Ottoman Empire.

On her own initiative, she sought out those who she felt could best achieve this task. In Maitiú's brewery office she summoned and assembled her company. In her mind, she knew she wanted soldiers who best knew the tactics and the culture of the Infidels. She sent for Dónal de Faoite, Mario Rossi and Sebastian Cardoso, late of the Papal Army. She hired the best swordsman, Teague Seaton, the most courageous soldier she knew and Craig Melville, both on furlough from the Queen's Guard and with the ready permission of Her Royal Majesty. The Chattan Confederacy was indeed a powerful entity in Scotland. There was no opposition from neither Argyll nor Bothwell for this venture.

After a keg of special Irish Red Ale was tapped and introductions were made, Meg chaired the wee assembly with the authority that only a Highland woman could summon.

"I have the authority and the funds to back this expedition. I be choosin' who goes and who commands. Be that understood?"

Captains Melville and Seaton glanced at one another, certain that either one of them would be chosen.

Meg continued, "Dónal de Faoite will command with Seaton and Melville as his seconds. Rossi and Cardoso will accompany. We will need the language skills of Rossi and Cardoso, the fighting prowess of Dónal, Seaton and Melville. Maitiú, Heber will need your friendship if his captivity has damaged his spirit, so I be askin' you to go too."

"Tá cinnte, Meg."

Pausing again, Meg said, "Are we all agreed?"

Dónal spoke first, "'Tis honored I am to be chosen to lead, but how will Sirs Seaton and Melville of Her Majesty's Guard agree to follow meself who be so young? And how will I be able to give orders to me own Da, for Christ's sake?"

Melville replied first. "Before I became Captain, I was a guard and remember well how to take orders as well as give them. For the love of Heber, I be yer man son!"

Teague spoke next, slowly and with measure.

"Normally, I would object if it were Scotland. But I be goin' to another part of the world and have been a teacher long enough ta know I can learn from

158

anyone. Dónal, ya have me complete support."

Cardoso and Rossi had no objections or hesitation as they had served with Dónal in the Italian peninsula and Morocco. Everyone turned and looked at Maitiú.

"A Dónal, a mhic, a ghrá, mo chroí, under my roof and in regards to our family, I am your master and commander. But in Constantinople we'll nay be under me roof. You are the son I raised to be a man. 'Tis a fine man you are. 'Tis that man I will follow."

The company all yipped in agreement. Now Dónal had to plan the expedition.

"We are not going to be able to march in and take my captain by force. We be but a small company, though fierce we may be. That fierceness will be needed and used when appropriate. Until then we will need to use stealth, diplomacy and bribery.

"Where are we going first, Captain de Faoite?" Teague asked.

"To Dalmatia, as we are going to find the family of that Saracen. I want to convince one of them to come. That might get our Heber out without a fight.

Down by the dockside at Dumbarton, Maitiú and Dónal made inquiries and discovered a ship that was due to arrive from Malta. This ship would be trading olive oil and spices for wool and cow hides, and then returning to Malta. Booking passage on that ship, they then hoped to find a ship to Dalmatia when they arrived in Malta.

With his small command, Dónal offered to help unload, load and then sail the ship back to Malta. This was to help speed the departure and save money that they may need in the future to bribe the appropriate people or to cover the costs of any unexpected needs.

Days spent by the docks waiting for the ship involved language lessons from Cardoso and Rossi, and sword lessons and sparing from Teague and Sir Craig. When the ship finally arrived, it was on a Thursday morning with the tide. As it pulled in, the company waited as the passengers left the ship. The passengers were as exotic as the spices in the hold. There were men dressed in strange clothing, some of it brightly colored. One could hear the babble of half a dozen strange languages.

Dónal was about to board to assess the cargo while the captain, the harbor master and the customs agent began to bicker over whatever captains, custom agents, and harbor masters bickered about. Dónal heard a loud, booming voice coming from a big man dressed in a brown monk's cloak who was just disembarking. The voice froze him instantly in his tracks.

"Féach, de Faoite!"

Dónal snapped to attention. On the docks below Cardoso and Rossi also snapped to as well. Seeing his son's sudden change in posture Maitiú looked upon the robed figure and his eyes went wide.

"Well I'll be a son of a bitch! We were coming to find you ya rotten gobshite, and it be you who found us first!"

With that Maitiú, Dónal, Mario, and Sebastian all ran to Heber—for it was Heber!—for a massive embrace as one might see on a Clonmel peil pitch. Heber was back and on his own. After all the flurry and fáiltes and pats on the back, Sirs Craig and Teague calmly approached and quietly shook the big man's hand.

Teague, with a smile, said, "Dónal Óg has made me in charge of ten sovereigns of Chattan gold. It was to buy you back if need be. Shall we give it back?"

Craig asked, "Shall I go fetch Meg?"

Heber grinned a most devious grin, "Let's take one of these coins and proceed to the Wycked Aye. I've many a story to tell ya, but can nay do it with this great thirst on me. Meg will surely find out I be back when she hears the celebration. Drinks are on me lads!"

Chapter Twelve

Father

The company had left for the docks almost a week ago to wait for a merchant vessel to arrive from Malta. It was so very quiet at the tavern with them gone. Maureen missed Maitiú and Dónal, she even missed the Italian.

Faolan had returned to Edinburgh. He had stayed in the shire only long enough to rest his horse and regain his energy from the long journey. He seemed distant on his return. They never managed to have any time alone. The time they did have was always in the company of the tavern folk. They laughed and they danced but nothing more.

Meg had returned to the tavern. The journey to Badenoch had taken its toll, yet she accomplished what she set out to do, and now a fine, skilled group of soldiers waited for the ship that would take them to Heber and bring him home.

Maureen had spent most of her time working at the tavern, keeping Philip company, and going to chapel. She had shared the news of Heber with

Father Desmond. Father said he knew everything would work out fine and that God would never let anything happen to a good man like Heber MacPherson. She hoped he was right.

But she had other reasons for her extra time at chapel that she did not share with Father Desmond. Her gift of sight weighed heavy on her mind. She did not understand the things she was seeing. Was this a gift from God or a curse? The vision of Katie had come to her two more times since the day at the stables, always the same image—Katie standing on the shoreline in front of the castle reaching out to her. She feared something was wrong, but what? There had been no news of any kind of conflicts or clan wars on the Isle of Skye, but it would take a very long time for such news to reach the lower Highlands. Maureen did not know if she should share this vision with Philip. Philip loved Katie and if he thought for one moment she was in danger he would be on a ship to Skye to retrieve her. Besides, what if she was wrong? What if she was not seeing clearly? She needed guidance. She needed Shalynn.

The next day brought clear, sunny skies. There was something different about the day, a feeling in the air, all seemed peaceful and happy. She finished with the horses and decided to take Olaf for a ride out to the loch for a swim. She would have just enough time before she was due at the tavern for the evening shift. There was a small cove on the back side of the loch, somewhat secluded. The water was calm, a bit warmer and perfect for swimming.

When Maureen and Olaf arrived, she wasted no time. She undressed and put her clothes on a rock next to the edge of the water and dove in. The water was glorious, brisk, but glorious. She had been in the water for about a half hour and was getting ready to get out when she heard a horse approaching.

"Well, aren't ya a sight to see."

"William Macaulay! What the bloody hell are you doin' here?"

"'Twas such a lovely day, I thought I would see if ya wanted to go for a ride. Went by the stable and saw Olaf was gone, so I figured you would be here. And here you are, in all your glory." He hopped down off his horse and walked toward the water, pulling his shirt over his head. He pulled off his boots and dropped them on the shore with his shirt.

"What are ya doin' William? Ya can nay come in here!"

"Why not? The water looks fine and I feel like a swim as well." Dear God, Maureen did not know what to do. This would land her in confession for the rest of her days.

"William stop, please. Ya can nay come in, I be…"

"Ya be what? Buck arse naked?" And with that he dropped his kilt and dove in the water. She swam as fast as she could to the edge of the cove and the rock where her clothes were waiting. She pulled Olaf in front of her and quickly donned her blouse and bloomers. As she pulled on her skirts and bodice, she peeked beneath Olaf's neck to see William swimming to shore. She should have turned around, but she just couldn't help herself. As she watched him walk out of the water, it was very clear that the good Lord had certainly smiled on William

164

Macaulay. She waited behind Olaf until he was dressed, and then walked over to him with Olaf in tow.

"Ya should nay have done that William."

"Do nay go getting' yer bloomers in a bunch lass. There be nothin' wrong with having a swim with a friend."

"Well, I do nay think we be that kind of friends."

"Aren't we now?"

"Nay, we are not! Come on, let's be headin' back to the shire. I need to get to the tavern and to work." He laced his fingers together and gave her a foot-up on to Olaf.

He rested his arm on the back of her saddle, "I meant no harm lass, if I offended ya, I be truly sorry."

Maureen looked down at him and put her hand on his shoulder, "I be not offended William, it be alright. Come now, let's be headin' back."

Their ride back from the loch was quiet, which was unusual for her and William. They always had something to talk about, but now conversation seemed a bit strained. His diving into the loch was a bold move, one she had not expected. They were friends, they were just friends…weren't they?

Maureen made it to the tavern in record time. The swim in the loch and the ride with William had invigorated her. Everyone was there and she had plenty of time to visit before starting her work for the evening. Fiona was fluttering between tables and singing one of her little songs as usual. Sara was busy behind the bar. Maureen checked in with Isabella for her night's assignment.

"I need ya in the kitchen and pantry tonight lass. Master Thomas brought in a full lamb and there be venison to cut as well. Ya be better with a knife than the other lasses and Thomas needs the help." It was true. She did have some skill with a blade, and knew her way around game and livestock.

"Thomas be waitin' for ya, off ya go now."

She nodded to Isabella and headed to the pantry at the back of the tavern.

"Good marrow Master Thomas. Tánaiste sent me back to help ya. Looks like we have some meat to cut up, eh?"

"Well, for a lass whose man just left for Edinburgh, ya be in quite a good mood." She just looked at him and smiled.

"Grab yer apron girl and roll up yer sleeves. Let's be gettin' to it."

They had been working for an hour or so when they heard loud voices coming from the tavern. Thomas looked at Maureen and said, "Here they come for the evening lass, maybe we should put a couple of those roasts on the fire." From the back of the pantry they could not see who was coming and going from the tavern and they had no idea what was going on. The voices became louder, and there was clapping and cheering. Thomas and Maureen looked at each other, "what the hell be goin' on?" he asked. They put down their knives, removed their aprons and walked out to the front of the tavern.

People were coming through the door, one right after another. It seemed like the entire shire was coming into the tavern.

Thomas pulled Sara aside, "What be goin' on Sara, what this be all about?"

Sara turned to him with tears in her eyes. "He be alive, alive and home. Heber be home Thomas."

The people began clapping and cheering. As they held the door open, the members of the company entered. First were Captains Rossi and Cardoso, next came Captain Melville and Sir Teague followed by Dónal and Maitiú. Finally, the big man himself, dressed in a tattered brown monk's robe, came through the door followed by Meg and Philip.

When Thomas saw him, he said, "Well I be a son of a bitch. Would ya look at that." Heber MacPherson had returned to the Wycked Aye Tavern.

When Maureen saw him, she could not believe her eyes. She looked to the heavens and said, "Thank ya God, thank ya." Her first instinct was to run to him. She started to move toward him but Thomas stopped her in her tracks, "No lass, no. It be not yer place. Mind yerself now, it be not our time. We have a job ta do, we just have ta wait."

Wait? Wait? How long had she already waited? How many hours had she spent on her knees praying for this man to come home? He was the one person who had shown her true kindness. He had given her shelter and a family she never had, and now she could not even go to him because of her station? It wasn't fair. She loved this man.

But Thomas was right, it was not long before they were all running their tails off trying to serve all the folks who had come to the tavern to welcome Heber home. Heber and the members of the company had been surrounded by well-wishers from the moment they came through the door. You couldn't get anywhere near them. Maureen managed to catch Maitiú's glance once or twice, but he was soon whisked away into the crowd.

Chieftain Sara and Isabella saw personally to serving Heber and the company. Thomas and Maureen were asked to return to the pantry, finish their task and get more meat on the fire as it was going to be a long night. Thomas put his arm around her shoulders and pulled her in tight, "Come on green eyes, back to work." He spun her around and they headed back to the pantry.

When they reached the door, she pushed herself free from Thomas's arms and turned back toward the great hall. Thomas snagged her by her wrist and pulled her back.

"No lass, you can nay do it. For your own good, mind yerself now!"

"I do nay give a damn about me station Thomas. I do nay give a damn what the merchants and nobles think. Heber be home. Maitiú and Dónal be home. Please let me go ta them!"

She tried to pull her wrist free but he would not let go. He pulled her close and wrapped his arms tightly around her. Maureen was wild with anger.

He put his head against hers and spoke into her ear. "Listen ta me now girl. Listen! We all be servants of this tavern, Heber's tavern, and a fine tavern it is indeed. Ya go runnin' out there now, ya do nothin' but dishonor Heber and Chieftain Sara. That be what ya want?" Maureen began to calm down and stopped struggling in his arms.

His words were true; she dropped her arms to her sides, buried her face in his chest and surrendered her fight.

168

"'Tis not fair Thomas. 'Tis just not fair."

"I can nay argue with that lass, but these be our stations. In all truth, 'tis not that bad, now is it? Besides, if I let you go runnin' out there now, the Tánaiste will have me head. I be endin' up sleepin' with the goats." That made her smile. "Come on now, let's be doin' what Sara has asked us ta do, and get these people fed." He took her hand and they walked back into the pantry.

The thought of not being part of the celebration, of being left out after waiting so long was almost more than Maureen could bear. She thought she had lost Heber and now he was home. When Maitiú and Dónal left with the company, there was the possibility they would not return. Now they too were here and she was stuck in the damn kitchen butchering a deer. Her frustration grew and she began to stab her knife into the venison roast she was trimming. The more she thought about the party going on in the great hall the faster her knife plunged into the poor helpless roast.

Thomas was watching her from across the table with a smirk on his face. He came around the table and handed her a cup. He looked down at the roast she had hacked to pieces and said, "So, ya decided on stew meat did ya?"

She smiled at him. Thomas could always make her laugh. He reached into a basket under the butcher table and pulled out a flask.

"This will make things a bit better," and he poured her a wee dram of whiskey. He poured one for himself as well and then raised his cup, "To Heber and the Wycked Aye Tavern."

169

Maureen raised her cup to meet his, "To Heber and the Wycked Aye." They tapped their cups together and then threw back the whisky.

The celebration continued well into the night. As the people began to leave and the tavern began to settle down a bit, Maitiú approached Heber.

"It's been quite the homecoming, has it not?"

"That it has, me friend, that it has," Heber replied. "I believe I've seen every single person who lives in this shire tonight. It be truly good ta be home."

"Well, ya have nay seen everyone yet. There be one who has waited a very long time for yer return. One who has prayed longer and harder than anyone for God to bring ya home safe."

"I know," said Heber. "Meg told me. Where be me little green-eyed wildcat?

"Not sure, I have nay seen her much tonight."

Heber turn to Isabella, "Tánaiste, where be Mistress MacLeod?"

"She be in the pantry with Thomas."

He nodded to her, patted Maitiú on the back and walked to toward the pantry.

Thomas and Maureen had been cooking and cutting meat for hours. They were putting the salt packing on the last of the venison when Heber entered the room. Thomas saw him first and tapped her on her shoulder. They quickly wiped their hands and turned to face him.

Extending his hand, Heber spoke to Thomas first. "Master Thomas me thanks to ya fer caring for the tavern in me absence."

"The honor be mine Heber. Sara's done a fine job keepin' us all in line. Thanks be to God for bringin' ya home safe."

"Thank ya Thomas." He looked at Maureen and then back to Thomas, "Will ya give us a moment, Thomas?"

Thomas put hand a on her shoulder, bowed his head to Heber and then left the kitchen. Maureen could feel the tears welling up in her eyes. Heber took a small step forward.

"How are ya me girl? Meg told me about all the time ya spent at chapel on my behalf, I want to thank ya for that."

She could barely speak. "Thank God yer home Heber, I missed ya so much. I...I thought you were dead."

"I thought I was too, lass. It be nothin' short of a miracle." Maureen slowly walked toward him and he opened his arms to her.

"Come here me girl." She fell into his arms and began to cry. "It be all right now lass, everything be alright."

She put her arms around his neck and whispered, "Welcome home...father."

He tightened his embraced for a moment longer and then he said, "Come on now, it be time fer ya to get out of this kitchen and have some fun. Let's be getting' an ale and joinin' the others.

They turned to see Maitiú and Philip standing at the pantry door with tankards in their hands. Heber was right, everything was alright now.

By the time Maureen got back to her cottage she was completely exhausted. Between butchering half a deer, cooking all night and Heber's return, she had not an ounce of energy left in her body. It was far too late to strike a fire. She changed into her chemise and crawled under the covers of her bed for what she hoped would be a deep and restful sleep.

Chapter Thirteen

Skye

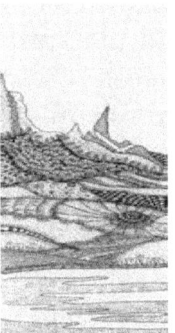

Pinterest.com

The sorely needed sleep Maureen so desperately longed for was not to be had. For although Heber and the company were all home and safe, there was still Katie. The image of Katie standing on the shore haunted Maureen's dreams. Something was wrong, she just knew it. She had been sleeping for only a few hours when a vision of Katie jolted her from her sleep. She sat up, gasping for breath. She saw Katie running toward the water. There was fire and smoke, and then Katie's face, so frightened, running in fear. Maureen awoke in a cold sweat. The sun was just coming up and she knew there was no use in trying to go back to sleep. She knew then, that she had to tell Philip.

The tavern was a disaster. After every big gathering there was always a mess to clean up, but this was beyond belief. When Fiona and Maureen walked through the door both their mouths dropped open in shock. Chieftain Sara and Isabella were standing in the middle of the great hall, speechless.

There were tables overturned, ale tankards everywhere, food and ale spilled all over the floor. There were some pieces of clothing scattered here and there, and even a couple of people sleeping by the fire.

The two girls carefully walked toward Sara, lifting up the hems of their skirts and stepping over the trash on the floor.

"My God Sara, what happened? It was nay like this when we left last night. I've never seen such a mess in the tavern."

"Nor have I Maureen. Fiona, be a dear and go rouse Detta and Maggie. See if they can come in early. Maureen, I be givin' you the pleasure of seein' those two gents out the door." She pointed to the two men by the fireplace.

"Would be me pleasure indeed, Chieftain." Maureen approached the two men and gave them each a firm rap on the head. They both stirred from their inebriated slumber and looked up at her.

"Good marrow gents. I be sorry to inform ya that the party be over now. Ya do nay have to go home, but ya can nay stay here. Come on, on yer feet now. Out ya go." They staggered to their feet and she led them to the door. When she closed the door behind them, Sara just looked at her and shook her head.

Isabella had not said a word. When the women left the tavern last night, they left the establishment in the keep of Heber and Thomas. Maureen had a feeling they both owed the Tánaiste a good explanation for the condition of her tavern.

The girls got the fires up and the water on to boil as they had many tankards to clean and linens to wash. Elena took the venison roast Maureen had hacked to pieces the night before and turned it into a respectable venison stew. It was clear to Maureen, as she was sweeping the floors, that whatever had gone on in the tavern late last night involved gambling. There were coins scattered all over the floor. By the time she was done, she had eight pieces of silver and two pieces of gold. She took the coins to Sarah who put them in the cashbox.

"Men and their games," Sara said. "What do ya think it was Maureen, boxing or wrestling?"

"I'd have to say boxing Chieftain that would explain the shirts on the floor."

"Aye, they had a good time indeed and they drank their fill as well. We be down to one barrel of ale. Here, take one of the pieces of gold to the brewery and have the Irishman replace the two empty barrels. He can put the extra money on the tavern's ledger." Sara handed her the piece of gold, "Do nay be losin' track of time now lass, I need ya back straight away."

Maureen grabbed her cloak and headed for the door. Heber and Thomas were coming in just as she was leaving. "Good Marrow Heber, Thomas," she said as she properly bowed to them both.

"Where ya off to lass?" asked Heber.

"To the brewery office to get more ale."

"Ah, well do nay tarry too long, I need to speak with ya when ya return."

She nodded to him in acknowledgement and said, "Oh and Heber, Tánaiste is looking for the both of ya... good luck."

They rolled their eyes at each other and then proceeded into the tavern.

Maureen was glad to be going to the brewery. She had not seen Philip so far and there was a good chance he would be at the brewery with Maitiú and Hamish. When she opened the door to the office there was no one in sight. She called out for Maitiú, then walked back into the brewery and found Maitiú and Hamish arguing in Gaelic over a recipe for ale. She cleared her throat to get their attention. When they turned to look at her, it appeared that Maitiú had quite a shiner and Hamish's lip was swollen. Definitely boxing, she thought to herself. Men, they never stop acting like boys.

"Maureen, good to see ya, what can I do for ya?" Maitiú came up to meet her. She put her finger to his eye and he grimaced.

"Aye, I jigged when I should have jagged and that bloody Cardoso caught me with a solid right."

"Honestly, Maitiú, how gettin' beaten in the face be any fun at all, I can nay understand it. And from the looks of the tavern this mornin', ya had quite a time last night. We be down two barrels of ale and Chieftain Sara sent me to pay for more." She handed him the fine piece of gold and his eyes widened.

"Chieftain asked that you put whatever credit we have on the ledger for the tavern." He just nodded his head and handed the piece of gold to Hamish.

"Maitiú, have ya seen Philip? I need to speak with him, it be most urgent," she asked.

"I have nay seen him. He had his fill of ale last night and took a pretty good pop on the jaw. I do nay expect he be up and about as of yet, but I be sure he be at the tavern tonight. The ship from Malta is still at the quay in Dumbarton. Captains Rossi and Cardoso have booked passage back to Malta. We be seein' them off tomorrow.

"Well, should he come by, please tell him I need ta see him."

"Aye, as you wish lass. Maureen, everything be alright?"

"I hope so Maitiú, I truly hope so." She said farewell to Hamish and left the brewery.

Considering the condition the Wycked Aye was in when they arrived this morning, it was looking almost respectable by the time Maureen got back from the brewery. It was good to see Heber sitting at his table, as if he had never been gone at all. The aroma of the meat on the fires and kettles of stew filled the tavern. It felt like home again.

She went behind the bar to store her cloak. Sara met Maureen and told her to meet her at Heber's table. She poured herself a glass of mead and followed Sara to the back of the tavern. Sara was already seated when she got there. She waited at a distance to be called to the table. Heber and Sara were involved in conversation. It took a few moments, but he finally looked at her and motioned her to his table.

"Heber, Chieftain," she greeted them with a nod and sat down next to Sara.

"Thank ya for joining me," Heber began. "I need ta speak with ya both of a matter of great importance." Sara and Maureen exchanged a glance as neither of them had any idea what it could be. He began to tell them what had happened to him while he was gone. He told them of the atrocities he witnessed and the pain he suffered at the hands of the Moors. How he no longer wanted to be a part of other men's wars or carry the blood of innocent men on his hands.

"I tell ya these things for a very good reason," he said. "Meg and I have decided to leave the tavern and go home to Badenoch on Spey." Maureen gasped in shock when she heard his words, as did Sara. He saw their reaction, "Let me finish now, if ya please." Maureen took a drink from her cup and braced herself for what was to come.

"The German surgeon who found me wounded, used me as an experiment. By the Grace of God, the hole he put in me head saved me fer certain, but it has left me weak. Me health is not right as it once was. I wish now to go home to me family and live a peaceful and simple life. But before that happens, there be a few things that need to be taken care of that have to do with the both of ya." He took a sip of his ale and continued.

"Sara, ya be Chieftain of the tavern now, and a fine one ya are. It be time ya be privy to a confidence the tavern has kept on behalf of young Mistress MacLeod here." Maureen thought, the gold and jewels—he was going to tell her about the gold and jewels.

"Heber, no, you mustn't," Maureen pleaded with him.

"She has to know lass." He looked to Sara. "Sara, in the cash keep ya be findin' a leather pouch with fifty pieces of English Fine Sovereign that be the property of the lass here. There also be a pouch of gemstones that have been sent to Castle Elliot for hidin' and protection. No one, other than Lord and Lady Elliot know of this."

Sara's eyes widened and she looked at Maureen in amazement. "So, that be what all the ruckus with Armstrong and yer Da was all about, eh?"

"Aye, it was indeed," Heber responded. Maureen sat quietly, staring down at the table, holding her cup in her hands.

No one spoke for a moment or two, then Sara asked, "But Heber, they both be dead now. Why hide it?"

Heber took a long draft of ale and said, "that gold was stolen Sara, stolen from someone of far more importance than Ian Armstrong and Robert MacLeod. It can never be told that it is here, never. Do ya understand?"

"Aye Heber, I understand full well," she whispered. She reached over and placed her hand on Maureen's. "Do nay worry lass, we be keepin' it safe."

"Now, there one thing left to do." Heber reached across the table placing his palm up, asking for Maureen's hand in return.

She hesitated for a moment and then placed her hand in his as he said, "Maureen, me little green-eyed wildcat, I take ya as me rightful charge and heir." Sara put her arm around the girl. Maureen stared at him in disbelief as he continued, "I shall see ta yer needs lass, and ya shall always have a place with Clan MacPherson. But the Wycked Aye Tavern has always been yer home, and I want ya ta stay on here under Chieftain Sara's keep. All of yer friends be here—it be where ya belong. But know this, ya be welcome at Badenoch anytime ya feel the need."

She could not speak. She had not the words to thank him.

He looked once again to Sara, "This too, we be keepin' between us. See to the lass's needs and try to keep her out of trouble." Sara smiled and nodded in agreement.

"Now, back to work you two. I have many to meet with this day."

Sara got up to leave. Maureen had not yet released Heber's hand from hers. She placed a kiss upon it and whispered, "Thank you."

He gave her a wink and a tilt of his head, and sent her on her way.

Maureen was so happy she could hardly contain herself. Until now, she was considered a broken woman, unmarried and with no blood kin. She had spent the last few years of her life as an outcast with no safe haven and no connections. Now, Heber had taken her as his charge and given her the protection of Clan MacPherson. She now belonged to him—a condition for which she was most grateful and one that would benefit them both. For no doubt, the gold and jewels would indeed be of great advantage to her and Clan MacPherson. She had great wealth at her disposal. But the fact remained that the gold and jewels were stolen from someone of great importance, and that someone would surely keep looking for them. The death of Ian Armstrong would not go unnoticed. Eventually, Clan Armstrong would come looking for her and the gold. It was only a matter of time.

When she walked into the pantry to fetch her apron, Sara gave her a big hug, "I be so happy for ya lass."

"Thank ya Chieftain, and I promise I will nay give ya any trouble. I be earnin' me keep as always."

Sara smiled and gave her a pat on the cheek, "I know ya will lass, we be just fine. Now off ya go." She spun Maureen around and gave her a nudge out to the tavern floor as if she were pushing her child out the front door to play.

It was mid-afternoon when Maitiú and Hamish arrived with the two barrels of ale. The tavern was almost back to normal and beginning to bustle with activity. Maureen was so consumed with thoughts of her new circumstances she completely forgot about Philip, and Katie.

Soon members of the company began to arrive for the farewell gathering for Captain Rossi and Captain Cardoso, most of them sporting either bruised eyes or split lips from the night before and taking full advantage of the attentions and concerns from the tavern girls for their terrible injuries.

It was not long before Captains Rossi and Cardoso arrived with Dónal. After tonight, Captain Cardoso would be returning to Spain and Captain Rossi to Rome. Captain Melville and Sir Teague would be leaving for Holyrood Castle, back to the service of Her Majesty. Each member of the company was given a gold Sovereign for his service. Meg was true to her word. She told the men they would be well paid, and that they were.

The tavern was fairly quiet. Except for the members of the company, the girls who were still working and a few travelers, it was pretty much empty. Most of the shire folk had been there last night for Heber's return.

Maureen was happy to be out on the floor for the company's farewell, and not stuck in the kitchen. She was behind the bar when Philip came through the tavern door. Ah, he is finally here, she thought to herself. He gave a wave hello and joined Maitiú, Dónal and Hamish at their table.

Not long after, to everyone's delight, in walked Lord and Lady Elliot. Maitiú was thrilled to see his cousin Gwen once again. The last time they had been to the Shire was when the Queen came through on progress.

After that, Cullen had been summoned to court as counsel to her Majesty. Elliot land bordered England and Cullen's knowledge of border politics was very valuable to the Queen.

Everyone was in the middle of greeting one another when Maureen tried to approach Philip. She put a basket of brown bread on the table and tapped Philip on the shoulder. When he turned around to look at her, there was a dark bruise on the left side of his chin and his lips were swollen.

"God's teeth man, ya look like hell."

"Well, I might look like hell, but I won me bout," Philip boasted. He lifted his coin pouch and gave it a shake so she could hear the silver inside.

Maureen just shook her head and said, "Well, I hope it be worth it because believe me Philip, ya look like hell." He tried to smile but his mouth seemed crooked, and you could tell that it hurt more than he was letting on.

"Philip, will ya have some time in a bit? I need ta speak with ya privately. It be most important. It be about Katie."

"Katie?" he looked at her with curiosity.

"Aye, Katie. Please Philip, when things settle down, we need to talk. I have ta get back to work now, but come and get me later."

Philip nodded his head and then turned his attentions back to the conversation at the table. Maitiú ordered pints all around and a special pint of stout for his cousin, Lady Gwen.

As Maureen went up to the bar to fill their tankards, she noticed that Cullen was seated at Heber's table, as was Chieftain Sara. She had a good idea what their conversation was all about.

As she moved through the tavern serving patrons and cleaning tables, she kept an eye on Heber's table as their meeting continued.

"The jewels be safe Heber, as requested," said Cullen. "But Clan Armstrong be none too happy about old Ian bein' run through and strung up. They will nay be lettin' it rest Heber. Ya know that as well as I do. Maybe it would be better if ya take her with ya ta Badenoch. I doubt Clan Armstrong would dare move against Clan Chattan.

"Aye, ya be right about that, Cullen. They would nay be that foolish," Heber replied. "I have ta think on it. Fer now, she be safe here. Thomas, Braden, Philip and Connor all be here. Sara, see that the girl be watched until we see where this be goin'."

"I be seein' to it Heber," she replied. "Should we nay tell her? Do ya nay think she should know?" Sara asked.

"No." Both Heber and Cullen responded at the same time.

"There be no need ta alarm the girl," Heber continued. Meg and I will nay be leavin' fer Badenoch until after the new moon. We be lettin' things be until then."

Maureen watched as the meeting broke up. Heber and Cullen joined the members of the company, and Sara returned to the bar.

Maureen was on the opposite side of the hall clearing tankards from a table when a messenger came in. It was William Macaulay.

He looked around the hall and then proceeded toward the company. "Beg pardon gents, M 'lady," he said as he addressed Lady Gwen. "Master Philip MacAlasdair, I have an urgent missive fer ya sir from Skye." Philip came to his feet immediately and snatched the missive from William's hand.

Maureen was startled when she heard William mention Skye and she dropped the tray of tankards she was carrying. They crashed to the floor drawing everyone's attention. She knew the missive was from

184

Katie. Philip turned and gave her a hard look. She watched as he opened the missive.

Philip's face began to change as he read through the missive. It was clear that he was truly upset by the news he received. Maitiú came to Philip's side. "Philip a chara, what be wrong?"

"Katie, it be from Katie," Philip replied. "Clan MacDonald has moved against Clan MacLeod. They have burned two villages, and are movin' toward Dunvegan Castle. The Lairds are forcing the villagers ta go ta Dunvegan fer their own safety. Katie does nay want ta go. She and Andrew, they be tryin' ta get off of Skye, but the Lairds will nay let them leave. She was barely able ta get this missive out."

Philips demeanor went from concern to anger. "William, did this missive come by rider or by ship?" he asked.

"By ship sir. She still be anchored at the quay at Dumbarton, will be for a day or two. Then she be bound back to the Hebrides," William answered.

Philip turned to his friend Maitiú, "I be goin' after her Maitiú. I know it be a great favor ta ask of ya, but ..."

"Ya need nay say it a chara, this bogtrotter has yer back." Maitiú assured his friend and turned to his son. "What say ya Dónal? Would ya be up for an adventure?"

Dónal stood up and came to attention. "Aye Da, I be right there with ya. It would nay be the first time the Irish have come ta the aide of the MacLeods."

Maureen reached for the nearest chair as her legs went out from underneath her. It was true, it was all true. She had seen it as clear as day. Thank God Katie was alright.

William saw her slump into the chair and came to her side. Kneeling beside her he still towered above her. "Maureen, are ya alright?" He asked.

Before she could respond, Philip was standing before her. "Ya know somethin' about this do ya not lass?" He grabbed her by her shoulders and pulled her to her feet. "Tell me, what do ya know?" Philip demanded.

William stood up and put a hand to Philip's chest to back him off. Philip released his grip and backed away. Maureen sat back down in the chair. Philip pulled a chair up next to her and sat down as well. William stayed right where he was.

"Is this what ya wanted to talk to me about?" Philip asked.

"Aye Philip, it is. I saw Katie, I saw her." They both listened as she tried to explain. "That night Philip, at the Circle of Rowan, somethin' happened. I saw Heber. In a vision in the water, I saw him. I did nay think much of it until Captain Rossi arrived and told us Heber was alive. Then, at the stables I saw Katie in the water in the rain barrel. She was standing on a shore in front of a castle reaching out to me. I've seen her twice since; always the same vision. I have the sight Philip, I can see."

William knelt back down beside her and put his arm across her lap. She had not realized she had taken his hand in hers as comfort.

"When was this lass? When did ya see her?" Philip asked.

"The first time be at the stables when Meg and Faolan left fer Badenoch."

Philip sat back in his chair and looked at her with disappointment in his eyes. "But that be over a month ago. Why did ya nay tell me lass?"

Maureen tightened her grasp on William's hand. "I be so sorry Philip. I know I shoulda told ya, but I was nay sure of what I was seein'. If it be real or be only a dream. This be all new to me, Philip. I did nay want to alarm ya for no reason."

Maureen could not look at him. She closed her eyes and turned her head toward William. Had she told Philip of her visions a month ago, he could have sailed to Skye for Katie and Andrew, and they would be here now and out of danger. What good was this sight if she could not trust it—if she could not trust herself?

"Tell me girl, tell me what else ya saw." Philip prodded. "Think now, it could be of great help in findin' Katie and Andrew."

She closed her eyes and tried to go back in her mind.

"Think carefully," Philip directed. "Any landmarks, anything familiar that…"

She opened her eyes to look at him. "I have nay been back to Skye Philip, I be not familiar with the land. The last time I saw Katie she be on the shoreline, and there be fire and smoke. She be runnin' ta the water."

Philip shook his head in frustration, "That could be anywhere. Think hard girl, be there anythin' else?" he pushed.

She closed her eyes and tried to remember. There was the castle, the shore, Katie, fire, smoke and…the stone. "The stone pillar!" she exclaimed.

"Philip, there be a great pillar of stone on the hill standing all alone."

William looked at Philip, "The Old Man, she saw The Old Man," he said.

"Aye, that she did," Philip replied. "The Old Man of Stor, well done lass, well done. I know where she be now, Trotternish, on the peninsula. It be alright Maureen, I be goin' after her."

He got up, put a hand on her shoulder and said, "Never doubt the gifts of the forest lass. Ya should have told me of this sooner." Then he walked back to Maitiú and Dónal to make plans for the journey to Skye.

Maureen looked up at William. He stared at her for a moment and then said, "I knew there be somethin' different about ya. Me Da told me MacLeod women were different. Would seem he be right. Come on now, I can see the Tánaiste givin' ya the eye."

He helped her pick the tankards up off the floor and handed her the tray. "William, ya must nay say anything about this to anyone. I do nay want folk to think I be, well, touched."

He smiled, "I will nay say a word. And do nay worry about Katie, Master Philip and the Irishmen be goin' ta fetch her home. She be fine."

"I pray ya be right. Sadly William, I know what happens ta women who get caught up in clan wars. Most of the time, they nay be fine." He put his hand on her shoulder in an understanding and comforting gesture. "I have ta be gettin' back ta work now William, many thanks fer your help."

As she started to walk away, he called back to her. "Maureen, would ya like ta ride ta Dumbarton on the morrow ta see the Captains off?" he asked.

The next day was the Sabbath and Maureen did not have to be at the tavern. "Aye William, I would like that very much."

"I be meetin' ya at the stables then, after Mass," he said. She nodded to him in agreement.

He went back over to the table where the company was seated. He said something to Philip. They grabbed forearms as men do when they reach some kind of accord, and then he left.

Maureen took the tray of tankards back to the pantry for washing.

"Looks ta me like I be talkin' ta Heber about one young Mr. Macaulay," Sara teased.

"Oh Sara, William and I be just good friends, nothin' more," Maureen replied.

"Well, let me tell ya a little somethin' lass. That man there, he does nay look at ya as if ya be only his friend." Maureen looked at Sara with surprise.

"But Sara, I told Faolan I would wait fer…" Sara raised her hand and stopped her.

"I would nay wait fer Faolan Maureen. He will nay be comin' back here anytime soon. And if he does, he will nay stay. That boy be a wanderer and philanderer. Now William Macaulay, he be a good man from a good family. And he be right here."

Maureen suddenly saw Sara in a very different light. Until now, Sara had been her Chieftain and employer. Sara's words touched her as the kind and caring guidance of a mother. She was truly looking out for Maureen's happiness.

"Thank ya Sara fer telling me about Faolan. I would nay have thought…I woulda waited fer him and…"

"I know lass and I be truly sorry. But Faolan be no good for ya. Philip and Maitiú wanted ta tell ya. But ya know how men are about such things." Sara gave her a warm hug and then put her at arm's length. "Now, finish up with those tankards and then ya can go."

It was a beautiful summer morning in the Highlands. Maureen walked to Mass and met with Maitiú, Dónal, Captain Rossi and Captain Cardoso, as wells as, Mistress Isabella and Master Thomas. They celebrated the Mass together. Maureen lit a candle for her dear cousin Katie and prayed that she would be home soon.

William met her at the stables afterward and together they rode to Dumbarton quay to say goodbye to the members of the company. Many from the Shire rode along. It was quite a send-off indeed.

When the company arrived at Dumbarton, Philip wasted no time in making arrangements for passage to Skye with the Captain of the ship heading back to the Hebrides. Philip, Maitiú and Dónal would be leaving in two days for Skye to find Katie and Andrew, and bring them home. Philip did his best to persuade the Captain to leave immediately, but the Captain would not have it. Philip's frustration was apparent as he came down the gangplank from the merchant ship. He wanted to get to Katie as fast as he could, but now he could do nothing but wait.

The members of the company bid farewell to Captains Rossi and Cardoso. Captain Melville and Sir Teague rode part of the way back to the tavern with those who had come to say farewell, but then parted company when they reached the road to Edinburgh and Holyrood Castle.

The rest of the group rode on a bit farther and then decided to rest their horses near the edge of the River Leven. Maitiú, Dónal and Philip were down by the river's edge tossing stones into the water and passing a flask between them.

"Ah, two more days of waitin', Maitiú. I can nay bear it! Why did she nay tell me?" Philip said exasperated.

"Who tell ya?" Maitiú tipped the flask and handed it to Philip.

"Maureen, she should have told me what she'd seen." Philip tipped the flask and angrily chucked a rock into the river. "She should have bloody told me."

Maitiú looked at his friend with concern. Philip was a passionate and emotional man, and his temper had a short tether. Maitiú did not understand Philip's anger with Maureen. Maitiú looked at Dónal who shrugged his shoulders, demonstrating to his father he did not understand either.

"Philip, what are ya talkin' about? What does Maureen have ta do with us going to Skye?" Maitiú asked.

"The girl has the sight, bogtrotter. She has the sight. She knew Katie was in danger. She saw it and she said nothin'. Nary a damn word to me."

William and Maureen sat resting on a fallen tree and talked while the horses grazed on meadow grass. They were watching the three men down by the river. Maureen saw Philip angrily throw the stone into the water.

"He be angry with me William, I shoulda told him right away," Maureen said. "He's barely spoken ta me at all this day."

They watched as the men talked and drank. Then she saw Maitiú look up from the bank of the river. He just looked at her as if he was seeing something he had never seen before. Maureen knew then that Philip had told him of her gift.

The ride back to the shire was anxious as Philip's frustration with Maureen was clear. Other than that, it was a pleasant ride as they rode back through the beautiful green, rolling hills of the Highlands.

Philip, Maitiú and Dónal discussed their plans for the journey to Skye. William and Maureen talked about everything from horses to the tavern and William's trips to Skye.

William rode with Maureen back to the tavern stable and helped her unsaddle Olaf and brush him down. When it came time for him to go, she realized she really did not want William to leave.

"'Thas been a most wonderful day William. I be so glad ya asked me to ride along." They walked back over to his horse.

"Aye, 'twas a fine day indeed," he hesitated for a moment. "Well, I best be getting' old Molly back ta her stall." He bent down to embrace her and

Maureen went up on her toes to meet him. He was slow to release her from his embrace.

"When will I see ya again William?" She asked.

"I be comin' by the tavern on the marrow if ya be there."

"Oh, I be there for certain," she said.

He swung up into his saddle and pulled up Molly's reins. "The marrow then," he said.

Maureen gave Molly a pat on her neck, "Aye, the morrow," she replied.

He gave Molly a nudge and headed down the road. She watched him ride away and thought, the morrow.

It was dusk when Maureen finally arrived back at her cottage. She struck a fire and put a kettle on for tea. She put a small pot of lamb stew she brought from the tavern on the fire, and wrapped up in a blanket. No matter how lovely the day had been, when the sun goes down in the Highlands there is always a chill in the air.

She sat before the fire, watching the flames flicker. She thought back on the day and the events of the last few weeks, Heber's return, being a ward of Clan MacPherson, Katie, William—so much had happened.

She was sipping her tea and relaxing in front of the fire when a flash of light startled her from her chair. She bolted to her feet, dumping hot tea down the front of her skirts.

Standing at the back of the cottage was the warrior-fairy, Shalynn.

"Jesus, Mary and Joseph Shalynn, ya scared the shite out of me! Be there any particular reason ya can nay just knock on the damn door?"

Shalynn put her hands on her hips and glared at Maureen in disapproval for her rude and disrespectful greeting. When Maureen saw her reaction, she realized her impertinence and changed her tone.

"Me apologies to ya Shalynn, a stór a chara," she said as she bowed her head.

It was then that she noticed Shalynn was not wearing her usual warrior's clothing. She was wearing a dress, a most beautiful dress of fine white silk with long flowing sleeves. It shimmered as she moved from the intricate embroidery that looked to be cast of silver thread.

"Shalynn, yer wearin' a dress. Ya look quite lovely."

"You seem surprised child," she said as she walked toward Maureen with a most determined stride.

"Well, it just be that I have nay seen ya in a dress before."

"I have just come from the Fey High Counsel, we need to speak child." The tone of Shalynn's voice was somber. She walked over near the fire and turned to face Maureen. "You have realized your ability, yes?

"Aye, but so far, 'thas done nothin' but cause me trouble," Maureen replied. "Why did the Fey have ta curse me with this, Shalynn?"

She looked at Maureen with surprise.

"Your gift is not the doing of the Aes Sidhe. Seers have been born to the women of Clan MacLeod for centuries. Because you carry the blood of the chosen Irish, your gift will be much stronger than most. No child, we did not give you this gift. The women of

194

your clan gave this to you, and it is they who must teach you how to use it."

She walked over to the table, took the pitcher and poured water into a bowl on the table.

"You see in the water, yes?" She asked.

"Aye, but nay without the leaves of the rowan tree," Maureen replied.

Get them child, and put them in the water."

Maureen went to her cupboard and took the apothecary jar that held the rowan leaves.

Shalynn had pulled a chair from in front of the fire over to the table. She was standing on the chair waiting for her.

"What this be about Shalynn? Do ya know somethin' about Katie yer not tellin' me?"

"The situation on Skye is direr than you know," Shalynn said. "The Tuatha de have many powers child, but the power of sight is not one of them. The High Counsel needs you to see what they cannot."

Maureen just stared at her. She was dumbfounded, but she was also afraid. She took a step back away from Shalynn.

"Do not be afraid child, I will help you. I cannot guide your visions, but I can awaken the Fey in your blood to help you see more clearly. I can strengthen your power. Now, take my hand. As long as we are joined, I will see what you see."

Maureen stepped back up to the table and dropped the rowan leaves into the water. She looked to Shalynn and she nodded her head for Maureen to continue.

Maureen placed her fingers in the bowl and stirred the water to set the leaves in motion. "Now child, take my hand and watch—do not look away.

No matter what you see, do not look away." Maureen took Shalynn's hand as a light rose around her. It was just enough to light the cottage so she could see clearly. Maureen felt a slight burning in her hand. The same sensation she had felt to her neck that day out on the moors.

The leaves slowly moved to the edge of the bowl and Maureen began to see. She watched as a vision of horror unfolded before her eyes. Panic, fear and destruction, villages set fire, women and children dead, livestock slaughtered. Maureen did not want to watch. She began to shake and breathe too quickly.

Shalynn tightened her grip and whispered to her, "Courage child, courage, you must not look away."

Shalynn's light began to fade for the vision was taking its toll on her as well. The last images Maureen recalled were those of a great castle, a great castle in ruin. Then the water went dark and the vision was gone.

Shalynn and Maureen both stumbled from exhaustion. Shalynn's light vanished and they were left with only the light of the fire. She sat down on the chair and Maureen knelt down on the floor beside her. Their hands were still joined.

"Dear God Shalynn, this can nay be."

"What you have seen has not yet come to pass child, there is still time. Dunvegan Castle is of great importance to Clan MacLeod and the Tuatha de Danann. It cannot fall to Clan MacDonald. It must not fall to Clan MacDonald! I must return to the High Counsel and tell them what you have seen. You have done well, we are most grateful."

"What are we ta do Shalynn?" Maureen asked intently. "We must do something. Philip and Maitiú are sailin' to Skye, and Katie…"

"The Fey have always come to the aide of Clan MacLeod and we will do so again," Shalynn replied. "But I cannot see to the safety of your friends. That must be your task."

"My task? Shalynn, I can nay travel ta Skye." Maureen got up from the floor and went to sit by the fire. She felt weak and had a queer feeling in her stomach. She leaned forward, resting on her knees.

"Shalynn, Heber MacPherson has as taken me as his charge and placed Chieftain Sara as me guardian. I can nay take leave fer a journey without their approval. And I little think they be willin' ta give it. I be pretty damn sure about that." Maureen said feeling defeated.

Shalynn walked over to the fire. "I understand child, you can only do what is within your power to do." She cupped Maureen's chin in her hand and looked into her eyes. "But I will tell you this. The men who travel to Skye are moving into danger. I saw it as clearly as you did. Without your help, without your gift, they will never find the one known as Katie. You must find your way to Skye child, you must.

As she walked toward the back of the cottage to leave, she turned back to Maureen, "Do what you can child, the choice is yours," and then she was gone.

The sun was coming up when Maureen walked into the chapel. The sisters of the convent were just leaving from their morning devotions. She went to the commoner's side of the chapel and sat down on the bench in front of the altar. She sat for a very long time, watching the sun beam through the stained glass, waiting for God to tell her what she should do. She needed so many answers, she felt completely helpless.

She knelt down, closed her eyes and began to pray the rosary. It was not long before she felt someone kneel down beside her. He began to pray the rosary with her. Maureen did not look up to see who it was, she did not have to look. When their devotions were finished, she looked at him with tears in her eyes.

"Now, now, no tears lass. Ya worry too much."

"Philip be angry with me Maitiú. Be he not?" Maureen asked.

"Aye, he be a bit perturbed. But do nay worry, he be gettin' over it."

Maitiú offered Maureen his hand to help her off her knees and they sat back down on the prayer bench.

"Yesterday, at the river, Philip told ya about me sight did he not?" she asked. "I saw ya look at me as if I be cursed."

He smiled. "Cursed? Nay, not cursed girl, blessed." Maitiú started to chuckle and said, "Maureen, ya be talkin' ta a man whose cousin Gwen swears her horse was a Phouka, whose cousin Fionnula can tell ya what yer going ta do and say before ya know it yerself. I meself have seen enough on these Isles ta know that God has created many things we can nay understand. Philip and I have seen things on our journeys I can nay begin ta explain. Be grateful fer what He has given ya lass, and use it wisely." He stood up from the prayer bench and offered Maureen his hand. "Come now, let's light a candle fer Katie and Andrew, and pray we find them safe and sound."

They walked out of the chapel to a day as bright and beautiful as any day could be in the Highlands. Maureen was headed to the stables to care for the horses and then to the tavern. Maitiú was off to the brewery office to take care of things with Hamish before he left with Philip for Skye.

Before he walked away Maureen took his hand. "Maitiú, I pray ya be careful on Skye. You, Philip and Dónal, yer walkin' into danger. Things are far worse on Skye than ya know. I have seen it Maitiú, ya be careful now."

"We be careful lass, do nay worry over it. We be back before ya know it."

As Maitiú walked away, Maureen thought to herself, no a chara, ya will not.

As Maureen walked to the stables, all she could think of was how on God's green earth was she going to get to Skye. The ship that the men were taking was out of the question. It was leaving on the marrow and there would not be enough time to secure passage or permission for that voyage. The lads would be at sea for at least a week, if not more, depending on the stops the ship made on her way back to Skye.

She decided that she would ride to Dumbarton on the marrow to see the lads off on their journey. The dock masters would know when the next ships would be coming in. That would give her time to speak with Heber, and ask his permission to travel to Skye.

She finished her work at the stables in no time. When she got to the tavern, she found Sara in the pantry.

"Sara, would ya mind if I ride ta Dumbarton on the marrow ta see the men off on their journey ta Skye?"

Sara thought of Cullen's words about Clan Armstrong's vengeance for the death of old Ian. She did not want to alarm the girl, but did not want her traveling alone either. "Very well. 'Tis alright with me so long as yer not ridin' alone. Be sure ya check with the Tánaiste though. She be havin' the final say."

Maureen leaned over Sara's shoulder and gave her a kiss on the cheek. "Many thanks Sara." Then Maureen donned her apron and got to work.

She found Isabella by the fire with Master Thomas lifting meat on to the spit.

"Tánaiste, Master Thomas, I would be grateful if ya could spare me from the tavern on the marrow. I'd like ta ride ta Dumbarton ta see the men off ta Skye if I could?"

Master Thomas looked at Isabella shaking his head, "I do nay like the idea of her ridin' back from Dumbarton alone."

Isabella looked at Maureen and it was clear from her expression that she agreed with Thomas.

"Please Tánaiste, it be only a short ride and someone needs ta bring Maitiú's horses back from the quay."

Isabella looked back to Thomas as they finished racking the meat over the fire. She wiped her hands on her apron and let out a sigh. "Very well lass, I can spare ya fer the morrow. But I be feelin' a bit better if ya could find someone ta ride with ya."

"Many thanks, Isabella." Maureen gave the Tánaiste a quick curtsy and went on about her chores.

The tavern was busy and the day passed quickly. It was mid-afternoon when William came in. As he made his way through the great hall, he caught the attention of every woman there. He was quite a sight to see. He graciously smiled and acknowledged everyone who spoke to him. Little did he realize that his kindness and humility made him that much more appealing.

He was almost to the bar when Isabella stopped him. It was always comical to see the two of them standing next to each other. Isabella was not much taller than Shalynn, and William was well over six feet. It looked like a Fairie talking to a giant.

He finally made it to the bar. "Good marrow Master Macaulay."

"Good marrow Mistress MacLeod."

"What can get for ya William?" Maureen asked.

"Draw me a pint of Desmond, will ya lass?"

"As you wish, I see our Tánaiste had words fer ya?"

"Aye, she tells me yer ridin' ta Dumbarton on the marrow, wanted ta know if I could ride along with ya." Maureen brought William his ale, some brown bread and cheese.

"And, what did ya tell her? Maureen inquired.

"I can nay oblige lass. I be at the blacksmith on the marrow. Can ya manage bringin' three horses back with ya alone?" Williams asked. "I have ta say, I be a bit concerned over that one as well."

Maureen poured herself a glass of mead and helped herself to a piece of his bread. "I be fine William, truly. Olaf will keep Maitiú's ponies in line and Dónal's mare be no problem."

"It nay be the horses I be worried about," William stressed. "It be the ruffians on the road who would find it easy ta steal four horses from a woman ridin' alone. That be me concern lass."

Maitiú, Philip and Dónal all arrived at the tavern stables before Maureen. By the time she got there, they already had Hope and Grace saddled, and were packing their saddlebags.

Philip turned to her as she walked up, "And just what are ya doin' here at this time of the mornin'?"

"I'm ridin' ta Dumbarton with ya," Maureen stated matter-of-factly. "Ya do nay think I be leavin' these lovely horses with some gobshite at the quay do ya?"

She tried to make light of the situation, hoping Philip had put away his frustration, but it was apparent that he was still angry with her. He turned away and continued readying his horse for the ride. She looked at Maitiú and he just shrugged his shoulders.

Maureen began to saddle Olaf for the ride. She kept purposely putting herself in Philip's way in hopes of annoying him enough to say something, prompting some kind of conversation to break the silence. But he would not have it.

Finally, when she could no longer stand the tension, she turned to him. "I pray ya Philip, do nay put me aside like this. Ya know I love ya and Katie dearly and I would nay do anything ta harm either of ya. Ya must know that?"

Philip stopped packing his horse and starred off over the top of his saddle for a moment before turning to face her. "That I do lass. But I do nay understand why ya waited so long ta tell me. Ya should have trusted me more than that."

"I be truly sorry Philip. I did nay know what was happenin'. I did nay understand what I was seein'. Can ya nay see that?" Maureen pleaded with him. "Please forgive me Philip, please."

He said nothing back. Finally, Maitiú spoke up. "Philip, ya know boyo, you, me and Maureen, we do nay have too many friends as close as the three of us have been. 'Twould be a shame indeed ta lose one ta somethin' like this. The girl's put her heart on her sleeve, can ya nay find forgiveness in yer own heart?" Maitiú asked.

"Aye, I can," Philip replied. "When Katie and Andrew be safe, nay before." He mounted his horse and turned her out of the stables.

Dónal walked up behind Maureen and put his hands on her shoulders. "He be a stubborn one fer sure. Do nay worry girl, he be comin' around. Off we go now. We have a ship ta meet."

They all mounted up and headed down the road past the tavern. At the crossroad, there waiting on horseback, was Father Brian Desmond.

"Top of the mornin' ta ya, do nay mind if I ride along do ya? Thought I would send our brave lads off with a blessin'."

"Ah, ya be most welcome fer sure Father," replied Maitiú.

Father Brian paired up with Dónal, Maitiú rode next to Philip and Maureen followed behind. Well behind.

The ride to Dumbarton was cold in more ways than one. Maureen understood Philip's anger with her, but she did not expect him to deny her forgiveness. She knew now that if anything should happen to Katie or Andrew, Philip would hold her responsible. She had to find a way to Skye, now more than ever.

She thought about trying to speak with Philip again and then decided to let things be. She made her apologies. She would accept this time of silence as her penance.

The sky was getting cloudy and there was a brisk breeze blowing in from the sea. She pulled her hood over her head and wrapped her cloak tightly around her.

Up ahead the men were talking about their previous adventures and travels. Father Brian would sing an Irish ditty now and then. Maureen would see Maitiú turn around and catch her glance once in a while. But he did not fall back to ride with her.

It was not too long before they arrived in Dumbarton. The quay was bustling with activity as supplies and wares were being loaded on the ship bound for Skye.

Philip went immediately to speak with the Captain to secure their passage, while Maitiú and Dónal began to unload the horses.

Maureen tied Olaf off to a post and started to make her way to the dock master's office. "Do nay be wanderin' off Maureen, we be boardin' the ship in a bit and ya need ta be with the horses," called Maitiú.

"I nay be but a moment Maitiú, I need ta speak with the dock master. I be right back." And she hurried off down the quay.

Dónal turned to his father and asked, "What the bloody hell does she need ta speak with the dock master about? Ya do nay think she be tryin' to...?"

Maitiú look at his son. "Aye Dónal, knowin' that girl, I be afraid she would."

Maureen pushed open the door to the dock master's office, "beg pardon sir?"

"Good Marrow young mistress, what can I do fer ya?" answered the dock master.

"Could ya tell me sir when the next ship to Skye will be comin' in?"

"There be another merchant vessel due in ten days, next passenger vessel be two weeks out."

Ten days. The men would already be on Skye by the time she boarded a ship. But it seemed it was the best she could do.

"Would there be passage available on the merchant vessel Sir?" she asked.

He looked at her with a furrowed brow. "And who would be travelin' with ya Mistress?"

"No one sir, 'twould just be meself." She replied.

He shook his head from side-to-side. "Not a good idea for a young lass like yerself ta be travelin' alone, especially on a merchant vessel, 'tis nay safe."

"I thank ya fer yer kindness sir, but I have no one to travel with. What be the cost fer that passage?" Maureen asked.

"It be three crown fer the passage lass, but I pray ya think better of making that voyage alone," he warned.

She thanked him and hurried back down the quay to Maitiú and Dónal.

The men were getting ready to board the ship for Skye. Father Brian was giving them their blessing when she walked up.

Maureen gave Dónal a big hug. "Keep an eye on yer Da fer me now," she whispered.

"I will girl, do nay worry."

She then went up to Maitiú and put her hands around his neck to check for the cross she had given him. "It be there Maureen, and there it will stay," he said.

"May Christ keep ya safe a chara." She had tears in her eyes as she embraced him.

Philip was standing a few steps back. Maureen had no intention of letting him board the ship without saying goodbye.

"Good journey ta you Philip. Take care and do be careful," Maureen said as she walked up to him. She gave him a hug which he reluctantly returned. "Ya bring Katie home safe now Philip."

"I will lass," then he turned and walked up the ramp to the ship without saying another word.

Father Brian and Maureen watched as the ship made ready to sail. They waved goodbye to their dear friends as they departed on what could be a very uncertain journey.

Father Brian put his arm around Maureen's shoulders. "Do nay worry lass, God will watch over 'em."

"I pray ya be right about that Father, I truly do." Maureen replied.

As they began to ready the horses to ride, Father Brian observed three men lingering back from the quay. He had seen them earlier in the day when they arrived at Dumbarton, but had not given them any notice until now. As he and Maureen began to ready their horses, the three men began to ready theirs as well.

When Lady Isabella had approached Father Brian and asked him to ride along with Maureen, he did not think there would actually be any trouble. But trouble seemed to follow this young lass everywhere she went. He ran his hand across his saddle blanket to reassure himself that the extra protection he had brought along was still there. It was, safely tucked away beneath the saddle blanket, just in case. He thought to himself, *God helps those who help themselves.*

"Are ya 'bout ready Father?" Maureen called.

"Aye, that I am lass. Let's be on our way now. The weather seems ta be turnin' on us. We best be gettin' along."

They mounted up. Maureen was leading Hope and Grace, and Father Brian had Dónal's mare. They rode single file until they were just out of the harbor. Father Brian looked back to see the three men watching them closely as they rode out. The strangers did not seem to be in any hurry to follow them.

The men watched as the girl and the priest left the harbor.

"Are ya sure that be her?" asked the first one.

"Aye, that be the one. She be carryin' that doe-hoofed dagger. That be the little bitch we be after," said the second one.

"What the hell she be doin' ridin' with a priest?"

"Do nay worry about him," said the second. "Priests can nay fight. Besides we do nay need him— only the wench. Let 'em get a bit farther out, then we be on our way."

Maureen and Father Brian rode quietly for a while. She wanted very much to talk with him about all that had happened. But this was no time for confession and besides, how much could she really tell him? Should she tell him about her sight? Would the Church see her as being touched or worse?

She had always trusted Father Brian. In fact, he had been the only one in the shire she trusted until she met Heber, Katie and Philip, and Maitiú. But now Katie was gone and she had lost Philip's confidence as a result of her own insecurity.

Finally, Father Brian broke the silence. "I do nay believe I have ever seen ya so quiet lass. Ya be worryin' over yer friends and their journey are ya?"

"Aye Father, that I am." Maureen replied.

"I sensed a wee bit of tension between ya and yer friend, Master Philip, did I not? Maureen looked at him a bit surprised. She had not realized that Philip's agitation with her had been so obvious.

"He be angry with me Father." Maureen began to explain. "Ya see, I had a dream of sorts. Sometime back, I saw Katie MacLeod in a dream. She was in trouble Father. I did nay say anything ta Philip about it, just kept it ta meself. Come ta find out she was indeed in danger. Philip thought I should have told him about it sooner so he could have fetched her and her cousin Andrew home before all this trouble started on Skye."

They were coming up on the stone bridge that crossed a small stream feeding into the River Leven. The bridge was narrow and would not accommodate them riding side-by-side.

Maureen gave Olaf a nudge and moved in front of Father Brian. As they crossed the bridge, the horses' hoofs clip-clopped along on the cobblestones.

It was quiet on the road. The storm was moving in from the sea. Gray clouds floated across the sky casting shadows on the meadow. But they would be back to the tavern well before any rain began.

They were only about a half hours' time from the shire and the tavern. Maureen pulled her cloak around her as a chilling breeze blew past. She held Olaf back and waited for Father Brian to catch up.

When he rode up beside her he said, "Ya know lass, dream or no dream, what be happenin' on Skye be not yer fault. I do nay see how telling Master Philip any sooner could have changed a thing. Ya need not punish yerself fer it, it be not yer doin' lass."

Maureen did not know what to say. In a way he was right, but he did not know the whole story. He did not know about her gift. He did not know about Shalynn and Aes Sidhe.

They rode on a bit farther when Maureen finally said, "Still Father, I should have told him. His silence will be me penance, no matter how long it lasts.

Father Brian started to respond to her when he suddenly stopped his horse and turned his attention back toward the bridge. They were almost one hundred yards away from the bridge when they both heard the sound of horses' hoofs coming across the cobblestone bridge.

When Maureen saw the look on Father Brian's face her first thought was that William was right and these people were thieves, ruffians who were out to steal their horses.

Father Brian shouted to Maureen, "Let the ponies go lass, let them go!" She quickly pulled up Hope and Grace's leads and untied them from Olaf. As soon as the ponies were loose, Olaf began to get upset and restless. Olaf and the ponies had an understanding between them and Maureen knew what she must do. She pulled up on his reins and brought him to stop. She quickly jumped down and grabbed Olaf by the bridle.

"Run my beauty, run! Take the girls and run home Olaf!" And with that she gave him a sharp slap on his rump and sent him running after the ponies. She ran back to Father Brian and swung up on Dónal's mare.

"Who be they Father, what the hell do they want?" she yelled.

"I do nay know lass. They followed us from the quay. Hurry now, they be closin' quickly." Maureen and Father Brian kicked their horses to a gallop, but the ruffians were closing fast.

They rode as fast as they could but it was no use. Father Brian's horse was much faster than Dónal's mare. He was well ahead of Maureen when the ruffians caught up to her.

The first one grabbed her around her waist and snagged her off her horse. Dónal's mare took off down the road toward the shire. The other two ruffians pulled up their horses and did not pursue Father Brian. They assumed he would just run, a grave mistake on their part.

Maureen was face down across the man's horse. She did her best to grab at the reins and confuse the horse. She rammed her knee into the horse's neck over and over again. It did not take long for the horse to become irritated with being kicked in the neck. He reared up, dumping both Maureen and the ruffian to the ground. When the horse was free of his annoying riders, he ran away and did not return.

Maureen was dazed when she hit the ground, but had enough sense of mind to pull her dagger from its sheath and slip it into her boot. She stumbled to regain her balance.

Father Brian was nowhere in sight. She looked around to get her bearings. She saw the road and the direction toward the shire, and began to run. She had taken only a few strides when she was grabbed from behind. Maureen struggled to free herself but it was no use. The ruffian picked her up off her feet and shook her from side-to-side.

"Calm down lass, it will do ya no good." He yelled.

"Put me down ya bloody gobshite!" She screamed. He held on to her as the other two men approached. As they came closer, Maureen recognized one of the men. The face was older than the last time she had seen him, but she knew him well.

"Logan Armstrong, I shoulda known. You fookin' son of a toad," she said as she tried to lunge at him. He took a few steps closer and slapped her hard across the face. The pain was sharp. She felt the blood run from her nose and could taste it in her mouth.

"It be most unkind ta speak of the dead in such a manner ya filthy little wretch," Logan growled. She tried to lunge at him again. The men just laughed, thinking they had the upper hand on a weak little woman.

Father Brian had ridden back around and was watching from behind some brush and trees. He could not wait much longer or they would hurt young Mistress MacLeod. He had to go now before they did what he knew they would do to her. He pulled his quarter staff from under the saddle blanket. He crossed himself and began to walk his horse out of the bushes and toward the ruffians.

He was using the staff as a walking stick, and pretended to walk with a bit of a limp as he moved slowly forward. He needed the ruffians to believe that he an easy target to draw them in close.

As Father Brian came through the brush, the men turned to see what appeared to be a crippled priest coming to beg for the release of their prize.

He came within twenty paces of them before he stopped and said, "Please my sons, I pray ya, do nay do this. Let the lass go now. She be just a poor tavern girl. She means nothin' to ya. I beg ya, in the name of God."

Logan turned and began to saunter toward him, his first man by his side, leaving the second man and Maureen behind them.

"Ah, well that be where ya be wrong Father." Logan's tone was arrogant, "Ya see, she be worth more than ya know. This has nothin' ta do with God; this has ta do with gold. And I be terribly sorry Father, but I be afraid we can nay leave anyone around ta tell of it."

They continued to walk toward him, the first carried a pistol and Logan had drawn a broad sword.

When Maureen saw the two men draw weapons, she feared the worst for Father Brian. "No! Stop it Logan, he be a man of God! For Christ's sake Logan, do nay harm him," she screamed. She tried to free herself from her capture, but she could not escape the man's hold.

"Let me go ya rotten bastard!" she yelled as she squirmed and kicked at the man holding her.

The men were only a few strides away from Father Brian when suddenly he lunged forward bringing his quarter staff around and landing a fierce blow to the first man's face, dropping him to the ground like a rock.

Logan raised his sword and took a swing at Father Brian who blocked his advance with his staff. Father spun around him cracking his staff square on the back of Logan's head, splitting his head open and sending him to the ground.

But as Father Brian struck Logan down, Logan' flailing sword had slashed into Father's right leg leaving a serious, gaping wound just above his knee.

When Maureen's capture saw his leader fall to the ground, he released her and charged toward Father Brian grabbing him from behind, trying to choke him.

Maureen pulled the doe-hoofed dagger from her boot. There was no hesitation, there were no second thoughts. She came up behind the man and rammed her dagger into the middle of his back. He jolted and lunged backward releasing Father Brian from his grasp.

He fell to the ground, gasping for breath. He was not dead, but he would be very soon.

"Father, Father, are ya alright?" Maureen cried as she came to the aid of her priest. Father Brian looked at her nodding his head as he had no breath to speak.

"Thank ya for coming back for me Father," she said. He was struggling to catch his breath.

"Well, ya did nay think I be leavin' ya to these blaggards, do ya now? Come on girl, we must be on our way before either of these two come around."

Father Brian took one step and stumbled to the ground from pain. It was then that Maureen noticed the blood on his robes. "Dear God, Father yer hurt!" She raised his robes to reveal a deep wound across his right knee that was bleeding profusely.

She took her dagger and cut a length of her cotton underskirt, which she wrapped and tied tightly around the wound on his knee.

"Thank ya Maureen, and thank ya for takin' care of the one who jumped me. That was brave of ya lass."

She dropped her eyes to the ground, "Father, I've killed another man."

He quickly made the signed of the cross and said, "Aye, well, under the circumstances I absolve ya me child. Now help me up on this horse and let's get the bloody hell out of here, we can talk of it later."

They had only Father Brian's horse left. Maureen helped him up in the saddle and then hopped up behind him. He was losing a lot of blood and his knee could not hold on to the horse to steady himself in the saddle. Father Brian leaned back against Maureen and she took the reins around him. They began their ride home—wounded, but alive.

William worked a long day at the blacksmith and was looking forward to going to the tavern. He was anxious to see Maureen and talk with the other folks of the shire, have a bowl of the tavern's fine lamb stew and a pint of Desmond ale. He was walking across the main road to the tavern looking quite fine in his linen shirt, his great kilt and leather boots, when he saw Olaf, Hope and Grace charging down the road toward him. He stepped out in front of them putting up his arms.

"Whoa! Whoa Olaf," he yelled. Olaf came to a stop, as did the girls. William took Olaf's reins and began to look him over.

"Whoa boy, what this be all about now?" he said to the great stallion. All three of the horses were wet with sweat from the run, but none were injured in any way. They seemed fine, but where was Maureen? It was then that Dónal's mare came trotting up behind. He walked the horses back to the tavern stables, pulled their saddles and blankets and then continued on to the Wycked Aye.

When he entered the tavern, he went straight to the Tánaiste. She was at the bar with Master Thomas.

"Lady Isabella, Master Thomas. Has Maureen arrived back from Dumbarton?

"Nay William she has not," replied Thomas. "Why lad, what be wrong?"

He told them of the horses returning without riders.

Isabella looked at Thomas and said, "I be lettin' the Chieftain know," and she went immediately to speak with Sara.

Thomas looked to William. "So, lad, do we need to go after her and Father Brian?"

"Father Brian be with her?" William asked.

"Aye lad, when ya were nay able ta ride with her the wife went ta the good Father and asked him ta ride along. Ya be thinkin' we need ta go after 'em, eh?

Before William could answer, the door to the tavern burst opened and Maureen stumbled through with Father Brain leaning on her shoulder.

"Sara, Sara!" Maureen called. "Please help me, Father Brian be wounded."

Sara ran to the door. William rushed to door as well. He took Father Brian's weight from Maureen's shoulders then turned to look at her. Her face was smeared with blood as her mouth and nose were still bleeding. William cupped her chin in his hand to look at her.

"Are ya alright lass?" he asked.

"Aye William, I be fine. I pray ya, see ta Father Brian. He be weak and he's lost a lot a blood."

"Quickly William," Sara directed. "Bring him ta the back of the tavern. We be seein' ta his wounds there."

Thomas came to help, and together he and William carried Father Brian to the back room. Maureen began to follow the men when she saw Heber standing ahead of her. She quickened her pace and walked straight into his strong, comforting embrace.

"Ah, me girl, what have ya gotten into this time?" he whispered as he held her in his arms.

"Why will they nay leave me be Heber?" Maureen asked as she started to cry. She felt a great pain in her head and her nose began to bleed that much more.

"Now, now lass, dry yer tears. Go ta the back and care fer your wounds," Heber said as he put a kerchief to her nose to stop the bleeding. "When yer cleaned up, come back ta me table and tell us what happened." She nodded her head in agreement and walked to the back of the tavern.

As she walked away, Heber looked to Lord Cullen. They both knew that the girl and the gold could no longer stay at the tavern. They both needed the protection of Clan Chattan. It was time for her to leave the Wycked Aye.

Maureen walked back through the tavern to the room where Sara kept her medicinals. She could hear the bustle of people as they rushed to care for Father Brian.

He lay unconscious on the cot. Sara and Isabella had removed his robes and cut away his pants just above his right knee to expose the sword wound.

They were rinsing the wound with salt water and preparing to stitch it closed.

Maureen did not interfere with Sara and Isabella. She knew Father Brian was in good hands and would be well cared for. It was best to stay out of the way. Maureen went to the pantry and poured some salt into a cup and filled it with water. She dampened a towel and wiped the blood from her face. She took a drink of the salt water and rinsed her mouth. The salt stung as it swirled across the cuts in her mouth.

She walked out the side door of the pantry and spat out the bloody water. When she came back in, William and Thomas were waiting for her.

William looked at her sternly. "Who did this ta ya girl?"

"Ah William, ya need nay worry about him. Father Brian took care of that one."

Thomas poured her a shot of whisky, which she gladly accepted and tossed it down in one gulp. Thomas offered another, but she declined.

"Thank ya Thomas," Maureen said gratefully. "But Heber and Lord Cullen be waitin' fer me at the table. I need ta go."

Maureen reached for William and he took her in his arms. He held her tightly, placing a kiss upon her brow. Then he released her and she left in silence.

When Maureen sat down at Heber's table, he noticed the girl was trembling. He called to the Tánaiste to bring whisky to the table. He poured her another tall shot and insisted she drink it.

She began her story of Logan Armstrong and his ruffians. She told of Father Brian's bravery and of the man she stabbed in the back. She told them of Logan's words to Father Brian, and how they were after her and the gold.

When Maureen had finished her story, Lord Cullen looked to Heber. "Well, that pretty much settles it Heber. The girl needs the protection of Clan Chattan. She can nay stay here any longer."

Maureen looked to Heber. "Heber, what be goin' on?"

Heber took a deep breath and said, "Lord Cullen has word that Clan Armstrong will nay stop until they have vengeance for the death of old Ian, and recover the gold that he and yer father stole. Cullen feels ya would be safer with Clan Chattan in Badenoch."

"But Heber," Maureen replied. "I was hopin' ta ask yer permission ta sail ta Skye and help Philip find Katie. The Armstrongs would never find me there and..."

Heber stopped her immediately. "No! 'Tis nay ta be had. Ya will nay be going' anywhere alone and a ship be out of the question. I will nay allow ya ta go off on yer own lass, so do nay test me on it."

He gave her a stern but caring look. He was not angry with her. She could feel it in her heart that he was truly concerned.

Lady Gwen reached across the table and took Maureen's hand, "Do nay worry over it, lass. Maitiú and Dónal be like hounds on the trail of a fox. They be findin' Katie in no time. Ya can rest assured of that."

Maureen smiled at her as best she could with the pain throbbing in her mouth. It was clear there was nothing else she could do.

"May I go now Heber? Me head be poundin' somethin' terrible," Maureen asked.

"Aye, of course, go and rest yerself lass. We be talkin' more on the marrow." Heber placed his hand behind her neck and pulled her toward him, placing a kiss on her brow.

She got up and walked out. She was frustrated and defeated.

William had been watching the interaction at Heber's table from bar. When Maureen walked out of the tavern, Heber caught his glance and with a tilt of his head signaled William to follow her.

Maureen walked up on the hill behind the tavern. It was a place she liked to go to when she had things on her mind.

From the top of the hill, you could see the valley and their little shire on one side. On the other side was the pasture where the cattle and sheep grazed. And from behind, you could just see the edge of the loch. The heather was as high as your waist and would roll on the wind in beautiful waves of color.

From the hill she could see the clouds coming in—the storm was on its way. She thought about the lads on their ship. They would have rough seas for the start of their journey. Maitiú would be sick for certain.

She sat down and looked around at the peaceful beauty before her. It seemed that if she were ever to come to meet God it would be in a place like this. Not in a chapel, but out amongst the peace and grace of the world He, Himself made.

She wondered how she could be sitting in such a tranquil place, when her dear cousin Katie was in a much different one. Shalynn had made it clear that Katie needed her help—that Philip needed her help. But she did not have the freedom to go.

Heber denied her request to sail to Skye alone. But traveling to Badenoch with him and Meg could be a start.

She looked up to the sky and hoped that the good Lord would show her another path that would somehow take her to Skye, and to Katie.

She heard rustling in the grass and looked up to see William coming up the hill. He looked quite fetching in his great kilt. She watched him as he strode up the hill.

"How did ya know ta find me here?" She asked from her hiding place in the heather.

"Well, there be only two places ya go when ya sneak off by yerself and it be too cold for a swim." He replied. She smiled at him as he sat down next to her on the hill. "What be botherin' ya so much that ya'd come ta the top of the hill and hide in the heather with a storm comin' in? Me Da be right about MacLeod women bein' peculiar."

The sun began to fade in and out of the passing clouds as the storm began to move in. Maureen shivered in the breeze and wrapped her arms around her chest. William pulled his kilt from his shoulder and wrapped it around her pulling her close. He felt warm, warm and safe.

"So, are ya going ta tell me why ya walked out of the tavern? I did nay climb up this hill just ta look at the sheep ya know."

He was right of course; he deserved an explanation. "I know William, I know." As she looked at him, she could now see what Sara had seen. It was more than just friendship and she felt it too. It was time for her to trust him.

So, Maureen told him. She told him everything. When she was done, she said, "So now ya see William why I be so bothered. The lads need me help ta find Katie, and Heber will nay let me sail alone ta Skye."

He put his arms around her and held her tight. "Yer Heber's charge now, ya can nay go against his wishes, ya know that?"

"Aye, I do." Maureen whispered. "But if anythin' happens ta Katie or the lads, I could nay forgive meself for it." She paused, "Katie's me kin, I need ta go ta her."

They sat together quietly for a while and then he said, "The storm be movin' in, we should go soon."

The sky was now completely clouded and you could smell the rain in the air. It was time to leave the hill and head back.

"Tell me William," Maureen asked. "How be it yer Da knows so much about Macleod women?"

"Ah, well his mum, me gran, she be a Macleod." He replied. "She has the gift just like you. So, when ya told me in the tavern that night with Philip ya had the sight it did nay shock me too much. She still lives on Skye, just south of Dunvegan."

Maureen could not believe what she just heard. She leaned her head back against his shoulder and thought to herself, thank you God, thank you.

William unwrapped her from his kilt and they got up to leave just as a few drops of rain began to fall. Maureen helped him put his kilt back over his shoulder. As they started down the hill, she stopped and looked at him.

He stopped a few steps ahead of her. "What be wrong, lass?" he asked.

"William, I have a great favor ta ask of ya," she said.

He took the steps back up the hill to meet her. "It be no favor at all lass. I be takin' ya ta Skye, if that be where ya need ta go."

William saw her back to her cottage and helped her set a fire in the hearth. He did not want to leave her alone, but Maureen assured him she would be fine and that she just needed to rest. He kissed her gently on her forehead as the rest of her face was swollen and painful.

She changed from her skirts and bodice into her chemise and robe, and wrapped a shawl around her shoulders. She sat down before the warm turf fire and reflected on all that had come to pass. She thought about Phillip and Maitiú, and her dear Katie. She prayed the lads would find Katie safe and that they would all be together again very soon.

It seemed strange that when her mum passed and she left the Lowlands, she was determined to return to Skye.

Her destination had always been Skye. Something was drawing her there. Not just Katie, although Katie's need was dire indeed. It was something old and inherent.

Very soon she would leave the Wycked Aye with Heber and Meg bound for Badenoch on Spey. From there, she must find her way to Skye.

Skye was calling her home and home she must go.

The Adventure Continues in
"Journey to Skye"

.

www.ingramcontent.com/pod-product-compliance
Lightning Source LLC
Chambersburg PA
CBHW071837020726
47502CB00004B/1399